THE
MURDER
CLUB
MURDERS

THE
MURDER
CLUB
MURDERS

A Rupert Wilde Mystery

David Stuart Davies

First published by Level Best Books/Historia 2023

Copyright © 2023 by David Stuart Davies

Author Photo Credit: Kathryn White

First edition

ISBN: 978-1-68512-309-3

Cover art by Level Best Designs

This book was professionally typeset on Reedsy.
Find out more at reedsy.com

To Kim Newman – The Master!

Praise for the Rupert Wilde Mysteries

"(David Stuart Davies) breathes new life into the traditional British mystery."—Val McDermid

"David Stuart Davies knows how to write and how to twist a knife inside the reader's mind."—Peter James

"Dark but delicious."—Gyles Brandreth

Prologue

France 1916

Sergeant Edwards scrambled into the dugout shelter, his eyes wild with panic. 'He's gone bananas, sir!' he cried. 'He's waving a pistol about, threatening to shoot anyone who comes near him.'

'I presume you mean Collins,' replied Captain Sharpe with a weary sigh, rolling up the map he had been studying. 'Where is the daft sod?'

'He's bedded down at the corner of Kitchener Alley.'

Very well, let's go and deal with him,' said Sharpe, slipping his revolver out of its holster.

They found Collins crouched down in the mud, chuntering to himself and occasionally giggling wildly. On seeing the two officers approaching, his body stiffened and he held out his gun, pointing it in their direction. 'Who goes there? Bugger or bastard?' He gave a high-pitched laugh, his body shaking with dark glee. Edwards held back, but Captain Sharpe moved closer.

'OK, Corporal Collins, stop playing silly devils and put the gun down. We have enough to cope with fighting the Bosch without having to deal with our own men.'

Collins' features blanched, his eyes wide with suppressed fury. 'Get lost. I'm safe here. Me with my gun. I'm safe. No one can get me. Not you or those damned Germans. Leave me alone.'

Sharpe sighed heavily. 'You know that's not possible. You're both a danger to my men and yourself. I appreciate you're feeling a little stressed. We're all bloody stressed. It's one of the penalties of war, but, you know, we all have to cope, gird up our loins….'

'You talk a lot of bollocks, dear Captain Sharpe. Stressed? That's not the half of it. That is not the damned half of it!' Collins roared out the words, and then, suddenly, he began to cry, sobbing like a child, his chest heaving wildly. 'I want to go home. I just want to go home.'

Sharpe and Edwards exchanged glances. 'I think I can arrange that, Collins. I can see that you need a rest.'

'You can get me home?' The response was a desperate whimper.

'Yes. I can get you back home.'

Again, Collins' body stiffened, and his face flamed with anger. He shook his head vigorously. 'You lie. You want to court martial me. That's what you want to do. Court martial me and have me shot!' He thrust out his arm, which was shaking wildly, and fired the pistol. The bullet thudded harmlessly into the side wall of the trench. In an instant, Sharpe leapt forward and, with a fierce movement, grasped the soldier's wrist and wrested the gun from his hand. Collins gave a cry of despair and slumped back, his body sliding down in the mud, his eyes flickering erratically.

'Come on, Corporal, come with me.' Sharpe tugged at his elbow, and slowly Collins responded like a child, ready to be led away, the tears leaving streaks down his mud-spattered face.

Turning to Edwards, Captain Sharpe observed in a quiet voice. 'This one isn't heading for the courtroom; he's a candidate for the funny farm.'

Chapter One

London, Spring 1921

W hy do I do it? It's the perennial question. Indeed, why do I do it? It's not merely the drink or the drugs, although they certainly play a part in this damned farrago. I admit that, but it's something else as well: *it's me*. It's something inside of me—a devil or an evil spirit that has invaded me and drives me to reckless extravagance that puts my life on a knife edge. It's a compulsion, an urge to challenge the fates as though I don't care what happens to me. And yet I do care what happens to me, but I cannot fight this demon strain in my soul. In fact, some innate force within me bloody well encourages it.

These thoughts pounded in Daniel's brain as he gazed with misty eyes at the spinning roulette wheel. The click, click of the dice as it ricocheted from one slot to another was like repetitive gunshots in his head. As usual, when the wheel was in motion, the participants, shadowy figures beyond the lights of the gaming table, remained silent, their eyes focused on the revolving wheel. The air was heavy with cigarette and cigar smoke creating, Daniel thought, an almost surreal, misty gothic aura, adding to his own sense of unreality. Was he really here in the casino? Had he really placed most of his money on number seven because it was his favourite number? Had he risked disaster on a whim? Or was this just a dream—the result of too much champagne and cocaine? These disparate questions formed themselves into a ball, rather like the ball on the roulette wheel, and thundered around his head.

The roulette wheel slowed. The gamblers peered harder. Click, click... click. It came to a halt, and the ball slotted neatly into a compartment.

'Number nine,' announced the dealer.

Number nine—not number seven. Daniel gazed across the green baize as his chips, along with those of the other losers, were raked away and placed before a fat, sweaty-faced man in a white dinner jacket sitting across from him, looking like an avaricious toad. His eyes flickered with greed, and he gave Daniel a leering grin as he placed his arms around the chips as one might hug a child.

Not seven, then, thought Daniel. Despite the dire consequences of this harsh reality, his contemplation of it was almost casual. In his inebriated state, he was immune to the implications of the tragedy that was about to overwhelm him. He took a long drink of whisky and gazed at the meagre pile of his remaining chips.

'Please place your bets, gentlemen.'

Daniel gave a twisted smirk and moved the remainder of his chips across the baize to number seven. Number seven. Again. This time, he thought. This time. It's got to be this time. If not, he was ruined. A little thought sparked at the back of his mind—well, that would be an interesting scenario in which to find myself, wouldn't it? Of course, it wasn't a clear-minded assessment of the possible perilous outcome, but then alcohol, drugs and his inherent recklessness were working in unison on his muddled mind. A thin trickle of sweat ran down the left side of his face; he wiped it away with a sudden irritated motion. Now was not the time to sweat!

Only the fat greasy gentleman was left playing this game this time. The rest of the gamblers had retired into smoky gloom, licking their penurious wounds. This was, in Daniel's mind, a gambling stand-off—-a sort of gunfight at the roulette wheel corral. He gave a gentle smile at his cock-eyed analogy.

The roulette wheel began to spin. Daniel's eyelids drooped as he peered at it, the whirling thing which seemed to break up into a mosaic of splintered images.

Click, click, click. Again came that fatal sound. The ball bounced around the wheel at speed, skipping past the seven slot with each revolution.

Daniel took another slug of whisky as his slender hopes began to crumble.

The fat greasy man leaned forward, a rictus smile plastered on his face. It was as if he already knew where the ball would land.

The wheel slowed and then gradually slithered to a stop. The ball plopped gently into the number nine slot. Again. Nine…not seven!

The fat greasy man gave a gentle chuckle.

Daniel resisted uttering a moan. He held it back; it would be rather undignified. Instead, he gave a gentle shrug of the shoulders aimed at his smug combatant, and then, rising somewhat unsteadily, he left the table.

Once outside the casino, he slumped down in a nearby doorway and lit a cigarette. Significantly, it was his last. 'What now?' whispered. 'What the hell now?'

A loud, insistent knocking roused her from slumber. Hoisting herself on her pillow, she gazed at the luminous hands on the clock on the bedside table. It was two in the morning. 'Who the devil…?' she muttered, slipping out of bed and grabbing a robe. Who the devil, indeed? It really could only be one person: Daniel, of course. What fresh hell is he bringing to me now?

As she approached the front door, the fusillade of knocks was still booming away. 'Who is it?' she asked, fairly certain of the response the query would receive.

'It's me, Bolly. I'm drowning. I need saving.'

Bolly gave a grunt, a mixture of annoyance and despair. She unlocked the door and opened it. The dishevelled shape of her brother stood before her. The cliché 'like death warmed up' floated into her mind. He was green around the gills, with moist bloodshot eyes, a slack jaw, and had that hunched, wavering stance of a drunk.

'I've gone and done it, Bolly,' he said, his voice full of slurred self-pity. 'I've lost it all.'

She wasn't quite sure exactly what he meant but was aware that it must be something terrible—or why in damnation had he come to her when the ground was about to open up beneath him and swallow him whole.

'You'd better come in, then. We need to get you sobered up before we go any further. You're not in a fit state to pour out all your woes in a coherent fashion at the moment.' She took hold of his sleeve and dragged him inside. He obeyed meekly.

'Into the kitchen with you,' she said, adopting the tone of scolding mother to an irresponsible child. 'We need to get a gallon of black coffee down your stupid neck,' she snapped, pushing him forward.

Half an hour later, they sat opposite each other in the kitchen, Daniel having consumed several mugs of black coffee. He was a mite sober but, if anything, he looked more bedraggled and lost than he had done when he first arrived.

Bolly, stern of feature, took his hands, and said, 'Now, you stupid boy, what have you gone and done this time?'

Daniel took a deep breath before replying. 'I've lost it all.'

'So you said. Lost what all?'

'My money. I've squandered it on silly things….'

'Men?'

He gave a guilty nod. 'And gambling and…cocaine….'

She pulled her hands away and shook her head violently. 'You are the most stupid of bastards. You irresponsible cretin…!'

'I know. I know. I wish I were dead.'

'Well, it certainly would be convenient for me. Do you really mean to say you have lost it all?'

Another weary nod. 'Yes. I am in debt to several people, and I'm in arrears with my landlord. I tried to win some money tonight to help pay for what I owe, but I lost it all. Lost it all.' He rested his head on his arms and began to sob.

Bolly stared at him in despair. 'And why come to me with your wretched tale of penury? What do you expect me to do? If it's money you're after, you have certainly come to the wrong person.'

'I just need help.'

Bolly gave a heavy sigh. 'What a pathetic devil you are. Give me strength. God, I need a drink'. She moved to one of cupboards and took out a bottle of brandy, and poured herself a large measure, which she downed in one go. She grimaced as the fiery liquid slid down her throat and began easing the tension in her body.

Daniel sat up in his chair and glanced at the bottle.

'Forget it,' Bolly snapped. 'I reckon you've already had more than your fill of booze.'

'What am I to do?'

'I'm not sure. The middle of the night is not the best time to start formulating plans. We'll have to give some thought in the morning. You camp down on the sofa in the sitting room, and we'll put our thinking caps on tomorrow'.

Daniel nodded lamely. 'Thanks.'

Despite his troubled mind, Daniel slept well. Curled in a protective foetal position on the couch, dreamless sleep came to him swiftly and deeply. Bolly, however, did not sleep. She lay on her back, her mind raging with thoughts and ideas. Gradually, through the fog of mixed contemplations, she reached the notion that if she was going to help Daniel squelch his way out of his particular mire (and she knew it wasn't a matter of choice—she had to), then it would be useful if the machinations involved in such an endeavour gave her some pleasure as well, some enterprise that would benefit her also. As the timbers of a plot began to construct themselves in her brain, her eyes brightened, and her lips broadened into a wide smile.

Bolly was fully dressed and alert when she entered the sitting room the next morning. Daniel was still asleep, breathing gently. He was roused from his slumbers by Bolly's firm hand. He dragged himself awake, eyes fluttering open. And he caught the pale light of morning filtering through the windows, and reality asserted itself once more, and a tight knot formed in the pit of his stomach.

He was led to the breakfast table and force-fed bacon and eggs and more black coffee. There was no conversation while he ate. Bolly sat across from him with a mug of tea and a slice of buttered toast, her brow creased in thought.

'I feel almost human now,' Daniel said as he pushed his empty plate to one side.

'That will be a first,' observed Bolly. 'Now then, my lad, I've had a thought.'

Daniel's eyes widened in pleasurable apprehension. 'Let me have it.'

'As I see it, you can't just disappear and start again with a new identity as you have no funds for such an enterprise. And there is no way that you can accumulate a large amount of money reasonably or quickly by legal means. I cannot see you as a bank clerk or a farm labourer....'

Daniel gave a short laugh. 'You're damn right.'

'Don't sound so arrogant. Most of those poor sods who are chained to their desks or ploughing up the earth are decent, honest citizens who have more sense than to fritter away their inheritance on drugs and gambling.'

Daniel bowed his head. He was aware that he had to act the penitent for the sake of appearance. He needed Bolly's help, and he wouldn't get it unless he assumed a mask of contrition. 'You're right, of course,' he said quietly.

'I usually am. Now, as I was saying, the only way for you to build up the old bank balance is by stepping outside the law. Doing something on the naughty list. However, I can't see you carrying out a bank robbery or shoplifting or anything as obvious as that.'

Daniel said nothing.

'So, it has to be subtle, something that suits your devious ways.'

'Like what.'

'Blackmail.'

'Blackmail?'

'Obtaining money by veiled threats.'

'I know what blackmail is. But who do I blackmail, and how?

Bolly pursed her lips, and her eyes sparkled. 'Have you heard of Ambrose De Lacy?'

Some three weeks later, Daniel and Bolly met and dined in a discreet restaurant in Soho. She passed over an envelope to him. 'That is a hundred pounds—a loan, my dear, to help get you started. I shall want it back when you have sucked the old devil dry.'

Daniel took the envelope and blew her a kiss.

'You are ready for this?' she asked, a smile hovering on her lips.

'Oh, yes. It will be a great adventure.'

'Maybe, but treat it seriously.'

'Oh, I will. A lot is at stake here. Believe me, I am more than ready and prepared to make certain sacrifices.'

Bolly's eyes glittered wildly. 'Good. He'll be dining at the Café Royal on Thursday. The best of luck.'

Daniel laughed. 'Luck won't enter into it.'

Chapter Two

Two Months Later

'Checkmate!' Kishen laughed with delight and sat back in his chair. 'You devil!' cried Rupert Wilde, with a broad grin, shaking his fist at his companion. 'You led me into that trap.'

Kishen's eyes sparkled with amusement. 'Of course. Isn't that what chess is all about: to confound and ensnare your opponent?'

'Sometimes it is wise to let your employer win,' Wilde added light-heartedly.

'I will consider it next time.'

'Not sure there'll be a next time if you're going to play like that.'

The two men exchanged comfortable smiles.

Wilde rose from his chair and stretched. 'Seriously, Kishen you're a fine player. It's good to be challenged by such a keen mind.' He patted his associate on the back. 'How about a cup of Earl Grey, eh?'

'Certainly. I will prepare a brew.'

'No, no. To the victor the spoils. On this occasion, I will take on the role of the gallant loser and thus will tackle the kitchen duties.'

'But that is my domain, and besides, you have no idea where anything is kept.'

Wilde gave a smirk. 'You are quite right. I would only make a mess, and I know how pristine and organised you keep things. Off you go then.'

Kishen returned the smirk. 'I see that I am not the only cunning one in this partnership,' he observed before disappearing into the kitchen. Wilde lounged back into his chair, a gentle relaxed smile on his finely chiselled face. To the casual observer, he would appear to be an indolent wealthy young man, like so many of the carefree and careless creatures that were now emerging in society after the dark days of the Great War. Smartly attired and graceful of gesture but seeming to have little drive or determination. But the casual observer would be wrong. That insouciant pose was quite natural to Wilde; it was without artifice, innocently camouflaging a sharp and intelligent mind and a courageous nature. He gave a gentle sigh of pleasure. He allowed his mind to wander back over his recent history. On leaving the army in 1918 after serving his country with honour, he'd had no notion of what to do with his life. He was without any particular focus or ambition. Somewhat fatigued and mentally weary after the war, he drifted. His inheritance allowed him to become a bachelor at large, but he wasn't content with the indolent life; it was just that he didn't know what to do with it. And then, following a series of unforeseen incidents, including securing a friendship with Kishen Chabra, after rescuing him from ambush by a gang of thugs, Wilde had discovered that he had a talent for solving crimes and so here he was a few years later, working successfully as a private detective with Kishen as his associate. It seemed to Wilde that he had indeed found his niche and a purpose in life, and it satisfied him greatly. For the first time in many years, he was content with his lot.

His reverie was interrupted by the sharp ring of the doorbell.

'I'll get that,' said Wilde moving to the door. Before he reached it, the doorbell rang again with a shrill insistence.

'Tut, tut, patience is a virtue, don't y'know,' muttered Wilde.

On the doorstep was a strange creature indeed. It was a tall man with a lank bush of blonde hair, which was obviously false, a ridiculous wig. An opera cloak hung from his shoulders in a theatrical fashion, behind the folds of which Wilde observed a purple velvet jacket and a florid cravat. In essence, the visitor on his threshold appeared to Wilde to be the representation of a villain from a Victorian melodrama.

The man was holding a folded newspaper in his hand. 'You are this Rupert

Wilde fellow from the paper? Private investigator? He broke off and peered closely at the print and quoted: 'Mysteries Unravelled. Problems solved.'

'Yes, I am Rupert Wilde.'

'Good.' The man gave a grimace rather than a smile. 'I am Ambrose De Lacy, and I am in desperate need of your help. Someone is out to murder me.'

Chapter Three

Ambrose De Lacy was a man of many deceptions. There was his name, for a start. He was born Harry Potts in a back-to-back dwelling in the small town of Cleckheaton in Yorkshire. His father worked in a local dye house, and his mother took in washing. To him, they were dull, uneducated, and unambitious individuals. Harry disliked them intensely. He sneered at their acceptance of their mundane status in society and their lack of any drive or desire to raise themselves from the shabby commonplace to a higher tier. From a very early age, he became determined to rise above these lowly beginnings, shuffle off this moribund parochial coil he had been lumbered with, and make something of himself. Something important.

The first step on this journey was taken when, to everyone's surprise, including his own, he won a scholarship to the local grammar school. It was here that he was able to mix with a different breed of children: the offspring of the local middle-class snobs. Despite the fact that they bullied him, sneered at his cheap clothes and his somewhat effeminate demeanour, he flourished in their company and while they were indolent and dismissive of their own privilege of attending this respected seat of learning, Harry worked hard, learned hard and applied himself with vigour to his studies. He had the sense to realise that through education, he could start to make his way up the ladder of respectability. In particular, he adored English and thrilled to the plays of Shakespeare and Oscar Wilde and the stories of Conan Doyle and Robert Louis Stevenson. His own early literary efforts received praise from Mr Mullins, the senior English master, and as his time at the school drew to a close, Harry Potts had determined that he would expend all his energies in the attempt to become a writer, a spinner of thrilling tales that would make his name and his fortune.

However, these high-flying dreams were brought to earth with a bang. There really wasn't an opening for a budding novelist in the little provincial backwater of Cleckheaton. On leaving the grammar school, he knew that he had no chance of going on to university. Despite Harry's academic brilliance, his parents would have laughed at the notion, and besides, they hadn't the means to fund such a venture. Instead, he found himself working at the dye house with his father. He hated it with a vengeance, but he was not daunted. He saved every penny he could while spending most nights scribbling away in his room, creating his stories. When he'd polished them to his satisfaction, he would send them off to various publications in London: The *Strand*, *Pearson's Magazine*, and *The Bullet*. He likened the procedure to releasing prize pigeons from the coop. He saw them flying free with the hope that they would fly back with cheques and contracts. However, none returned with such promise. He received a few rejections, but in the main, he heard nothing at all regarding the fate of his tales. In a wastepaper basket somewhere in London, no doubt, he assumed. But the lad persevered. He was determined to leave the dye house, his parents, and Cleckheaton as soon as he could. He continued to burn the midnight oil creating his adventurous yarns. He saw this activity as a kind of apprenticeship. The more he wrote, the more he saw his writing style improve.

Then it happened. One of his detective stories featuring Marcus Brakespeare, a poor man's Sherlock Holmes, was accepted by a small publication called *Smashing Yarns*, a magazine aimed at the youth market. He received a cheque for two guineas. He hugged it to his chest as tears trickled down his cheeks. The cheque was a sign: he was on his way. When he received a letter a month later from the editor asking if he could provide further Marcus Brakespeare stories, he rattled off another one as fast as he could before drawing out all his savings and setting off for London, where he was certain that he would find fame and fortune.

He left home one foggy October night to catch the midnight express from

Leeds to London. He crept down the stairs and out into the autumn chill, closing the door behind him for the last time. He knew he would never see that door again, or the inside of the house, or, indeed, his parents, who knew nothing of their son's literary success or his plans to leave home. He had kept all that to himself. The house, his parents, the dyehouse, and the scruffy little town were now his past, to be forgotten and remain a secret.

On arriving in London with huge ambitions and very little in his wallet, he had already determined to change himself from Harry Potts to Ambrose De Lacy—certainly a more suitable name for a literary gent who was going to go far. He found very cheap diggings and began writing at a furious pace. His success at *Smashing Yarns* gave him some leeway for him to being considered by other publications. Rejections still came, but there were also the occasional acceptances which buoyed up the budding scribe.

One particular story, 'The Bicycle of Death,' featuring a new character, a female detective by the name of Lucy Dawes, was accepted by the *Strand*. The tale was a great success with the readers, and as a result, Ambrose De Lacy became a regular contributor to this well-respected publication. De Lacy was slowly moving up in the literary and social world. An improved wardrobe and the benefit of elocution lessons enabled him to fit more easily into his new life.

At a drinks party, he was approached by one of the directors of the publishing house of Hutchinson and Co. 'Love those mystery tales of yours featuring that lady 'tec. Clever stuff,' he said grandly.

'Thank you,' smiled De Lacy in return.

'Ever thought about turning out a novel featuring the girl?'

De Lacy paused for a moment, staring down at his drink, and then he said, 'Not until now.'

'We'd be very interested in publishing such a volume.'

'I'll have one on your desk in two months' time,' said De Lacy, his smile broadening.

And so, he did. *The Locked Trunk Mystery* was an international bestseller and Ambrose De Lacy, along with his bright-eyed heroine Lucy Dawes, became household names.

There was no stopping him now. Very soon, he was regarded as one of the most successful and popular of all mystery writers. The fame and wealth that he accrued from his writing allowed him to indulge in his passions of wine and young men. While his literary colleagues were well aware of what they termed his peccadillos, De Lacy was discreet enough to keep such information away from the general public. His secret homosexual adventures were another of his deceptions.

What really dismayed him at this time was the fact that as a young man in his early thirties, he was rapidly losing his hair. It seemed that every morning when he woke, there were more blonde strands on his pillow. In desperation, he decided to resort to the use of a hairpiece, a wig. He settled for a rather flamboyant blonde toupee which almost covered his ears and fell across his forehead. It was expertly made, but in truth, it fooled few observers. However, De Lacy felt safe under its blonde roofing, and he believed it enhanced his attractiveness.

As the new century made its way forward, De Lacy found himself a major figure in literary society. He was a member of two London clubs and dined often with other celebrated authors of the day, including Arthur Conan Doyle, Bram Stoker, and Jerome K. Jerome. A murder mystery by Ambrose De Lacy was a regular feature in the bestselling lists. Nevertheless, he was conscious that a writer of detective stories was regarded as being in the second rank of authors. Even Doyle, with his Sherlock Holmes success, had endeavoured to escape the label of 'crime writer' by extending his range of fiction into historical sagas. De Lacy had no desire to take this route; he enjoyed creating detective mysteries with locked rooms, bloody corpses, and puzzling crimes. Pulling the wool over the readers' eyes was one of his great passions. Unlike Doyle, he believed that his mission was to raise the profile and respectability of murder mystery fiction rather than escape from it. To this purpose, he began having thoughts of creating an elite club of the most successful crime story writers with himself at the head, which would elevate the status of the genre. He discussed it with a few fellow scribes, most of whom appeared to like the idea in principle but did not demonstrate the kind of enthusiasm De Lacy had expected. He realised that he would have to select his crew very carefully if the venture was to achieve its potential. There would be no room for half-hearted involvement.

Slowly, he gathered his members of what he had decided to call The Murder Club. He had also determined that the membership should restrict itself to seven, including himself. The Murder Club would be exclusive, prestigious, and famous. It was in essence a social club where writers of mystery novels and stories could meet and dine—four dinners a year—and discuss their craft, exchange ideas, and work on schemes to promote their books.

By the time the war ended, Ambrose De Lacy was a well-known public figure, one of the most popular writers of his day. It seemed that he could turn out thrillers and detective stories with speed and aplomb. He approached his craft in a strict, well-ordered dedicated fashion; the same could not be said for his private life. As the new decade of the twenties arrived, he was nearing his forties, and De Lacy had developed a strong desire to find someone to share his life with, someone he could love and cherish. He had grown tired of all the shallow affairs he had indulged in with pretty but vacuous young men. He knew that they were only with him because of his money and notoriety. None of them cared a jot for him personally; and, if he were honest, he did not care a jot for them either.

Then he met Daniel.

Chapter Four

When Kishen brought in the tea on a tray, he discovered that there was a visitor ensconced in one of the armchairs. He was a tall thin individual, with large restless blue eyes which radiated an air of arrogance. He sat with his hands in his lap, bony fingers entwined, shoulders hunched as though in an act of self-containment, giving Kishen the impression that this man did not want to reveal much about himself.

'We'll need another cup, old chap,' said Wilde. 'One for our client.'

Great heavens,' cried Kishen. 'It's Ambrose De Lacy, isn't it?'

De Lacy nodded. 'It is.'

'This is the famous detective story writer, Rupert. I am an admirer of your work, sir. I have read a number of your books,' Kishen said.

'Yes, I am aware that we are in the presence of a very successful crime writer,' said Wilde, 'and he comes to us with a mystery of his own.'

'I will bring another cup,' said Kishen, disappearing into the kitchen.

Once the tea ceremony had been completed, Wilde sat back and addressed the visitor. 'So, Mr De Lacy, please tell us about this death threat.'

Kishen gave a sharp intake of breath at this revelation but said nothing.

De Lacy reached into his inside pocket and produced a long envelope, which he passed to Wilde who examined it carefully, noting that it bore only De Lacy's name written a fluid and languorous hand. There was no address, and the envelope had no stamp. 'Expensive stationery,' he muttered. 'How did you come to receive this?'

'I found it on the doormat this morning.'

'Hand delivered,' murmured Wilde as he extracted a single sheet of writing paper. The message it contained was written in simple capital letters in purple ink:

YOU DO NOT DESERVE TO LIVE. YOU WILL DIE SOON. I WILL KILL YOU.

'Well, the writer gets straight to the point, doesn't he?' observed Wilde, passing the letter to Kishen. 'You've obviously upset someone rather badly. Do you have any idea who sent this?'

'Of course not,' snapped De Lacy.

'It could be some crank,' said Kishen. 'There are those who enjoy sending such missives to famous people with the sole purpose of unnerving them.'

'Well, it's certainly done that,' said De Lacy tartly.

'My friend Kishen is right. The act of sending such letters gives the writer a sense of power. Many are just harmless, but of course … some are not. It is interesting that this chap says you 'do not deserve to live', which suggests perhaps that he believes you have done something which has affected him personally in a detrimental way.'

'Like what?'

'Well, for the moment, only you can answer that,' observed Wilde.

De Lacy puffed out his cheeks. 'I have no idea. I know that one cannot travel through life without upsetting some people, but to the best of my knowledge, I haven't gone out of my way to hurt anyone deliberately.'

'There is no one in your past who might bear some sort of grudge?' asked Kishen.

De Lacy shook his head. 'If I could think of anyone, I would have told you.'

'Do you live alone?' asked Kishen.

'Yes. I am a bachelor.'

'Have you had any romantic liaisons that have ended unhappily?'

'What on earth do you mean?' There was strained anger in this response, and colour rose in the author's face.

'A spurned lover.'

'Don't talk rot!'

'Well, it is clear that your correspondent is someone who knows you and knows where you live,' said Wilde. 'Some kind of jealous colleague, perhaps.

As a successful author, you must have rivals.'

'Of course. I am highly successful, and that has caused jealousy and frustration in lesser talented writers, but surely none would go to the extreme lengths of considering murdering me.'

'Possibly not, but sending you threatening letters to unnerve you, to play dark games with your mind in order to put you off your stroke - maybe they consider that is all that's needed to exact some kind of revenge.'

'Revenge! Revenge for what?'

Wilde gave a casual shrug. 'For being so successful.'

It seemed to Wilde that De Lacy was about to issue a theatrical disparaging laugh, but his face froze as he opened his mouth, and his eyes widened in surprise as though a fresh notion had come to him. 'I...I suppose you could be right.'

'Indeed. Surely there are those who would be pleased if you fell off the old perch or you were unnerved sufficiently to hinder your creative flow. As I understand it, you are probably the most successful crime writer in this country at the moment and, as such, other players in your particular game don't get much of a look in. Not while you're alive, that is.'

The awful truth of this assessment was a shocking revelation to De Lacy. He had not thought of this before. As the idea sank in, his hands began to tremble, and all the colour drained from his cheeks.

Wilde responded with a gentle grin. 'If you wish me to help you, I must explore every avenue. Surely there must be one or two rivals who would be eager for you to topple off the best-selling lists, making room for them.'

Now came the disparaging laugh. 'Oh, they are legion,' De Lacy announced grandly.

'Could you narrow it down to a few names?' suggested Kishen diplomatically.

'A few names?' The author thought for a moment, and then with a dark smile, he said, 'Well, any one of the members of The Murder Club.'

'What on earth is The Murder Club?' asked Wilde, lighting a cigarette.

Chapter Five

And then he met Daniel.

He had been dining at the Café Royal with his editor, Simon North, who had left early to catch a train. Sitting alone, De Lacy did not feel inclined to desert the warmth and the conviviality of the dining room to step out into the rather sordid real world and return to the loneliness of an empty flat and so he ordered another bottle of red wine. Whenever he consumed a large quantity of alcohol, he always thought that the inebriation it brought helped to ease the pain of his loneliness but, of course it didn't. It merely masked it for a short while. The following morning, as his head ached and daylight and sobriety reminded him of the truth, he was honest enough to admit that it was a foolish fallacy—until the next time.

He poured a fresh glassful from the new bottle, enjoying watching the red liquid splash luxuriously into the glass. He inhaled the aroma momentarily before sipping the wine, allowing it to roll around in his mouth before swallowing it gently. With a sigh, he sat back to survey the room and to study the various well-heeled diners, viewed through a fine grey haze of cigar smoke. Those secure individuals, at ease with their own wealth, he thought. Although he was himself very comfortably off, thanks to his writing and healthy book sales, he never felt part of this privileged world. He was still too conscious of his humble roots in that grimy provincial backwater in Yorkshire. The shadow of the dye house and its implications still loomed darkly at the back of his mind, refusing to be completely banished from his consciousness.

'I say, sorry to bother you, sir, but aren't you Ambrose De Lacy?' The sharp clipped tones broke in on his reverie, and he saw that there was a young man standing close to his table. He was a tall fellow with lean, handsome features, wide expressive eyes, and a charming smile which broadened as he caught De Lacy's attention.

Before he replied to the young man's query, the author was already enraptured by this suave and attractive young man. There was such an air of freshness, elegance, and beauty about him. He was, mused De Lacy fancifully, like a flesh and blood version of Dorian Gray.

He nodded gently. 'Yes, I am Ambrose De Lacy,' he replied.

'Gosh, sir, this is such a privilege to meet you. I am a great admirer of your work. I confess I have read all your novels. I think they are absolutely spiffing.' His features flushed as he spoke.

De Lacy smiled at the young man's enthusiasm.

'Read them all? That is quite a feat. Well, thank you. It is always gratifying to meet a satisfied reader.'

'I say, sir, would you think it an awful impertinence if I asked you to shake my hand?'

De Lacy chuckled. 'Of course not. In fact, take a seat and share a glass of wine with me. An author is always in need of enthusiastic support.'

'Really? I say, that would be wonderful.' The young man pulled up a chair, and De Lacy summoned the waiter for another glass.

'Well,', he said, as he poured the wine, 'you know who I am, but I don't know who you are.'

The young man took a sip of wine before replying. 'I am Daniel; I've just come down from Cambridge, but quite soon, I'll be off to France.'

De Lacy frowned. More young fodder destined to fall in the mud of the trenches, he thought. What a tragedy if this beautiful flower of youth should meet such a fate.

'What were you reading at Cambridge?'

'Classics and Latin.' He gave a light, ironic laugh. 'Subjects ideal for dealing with the modern world. I suppose going to war has prevented me from tackling anything like a career. For the moment, at least.'

'What do you really want to do?'

Daniel shrugged. 'I have no strong desires. I do fancy my hand at writing stories like you, but I'm not much good at it. Luckily, my father left me a small allowance in his will, so I reckon I can take my time. But in the meantime, I'll be playing soldiers. I'm off to officer training camp within the month. Tonight is one of my last social flings before I slip on that rough khaki uniform.' He laughed again and took another swig of wine.

'That is a shame,' observed De Lacy. 'There is so much danger out there across the channel.'

'Well, my older brother is out in France already, so I really can't flunk it. But, you know, I reckon I'll be all right. For some strange reason, I feel I bear a charmed life. I think I have a kindly angel sitting on my shoulder. I have a vision of me as Old Father William at ninety, fat, white-haired, and standing on my head.'

De Lacy laughed. What a strange young man this was—and so irresistibly attractive.

'Who are you dining with tonight?' he asked, gazing around the room for a clue.

'Oh, an old chum from my school days and his wife. But we have eaten, and they've gone home and left me on my own. I was about to depart, too, when I saw you. I couldn't resist coming over to say hello.'

De Lacy leaned forward. 'I'm so glad you did,' he said softly, the underlying implications of the response not being lost on Daniel.

There was a silence. It was not an awkward one, but it was one that crackled with certain possibilities. De Lacy poured another glass of wine each, emptying the bottle.

'So,' he said in a leisurely fashion, leaning back in his chair, 'you have tried your hand at writing….'

'Oh, in a very amateurish fashion.'

'Fiction?'

Daniel nodded.

'What sort of stuff?'

'Oh, you know, mystery, gothic tales. All rubbish, I assure you. I just have to read one of your novels to realise how incompetent I am.'

De Lacy smiled indulgently. 'You should have seen some of my early stuff.' He didn't mean it. He was well aware that his early stuff had always shown promise. If it hadn't, he wouldn't be in the position in the publishing world that he was now. 'Perhaps you'd like to let me have a look at some of your work.'

Daniel's eyes widened with mock alarm. 'Gracious, no! I have nothing of any real worth to show you.'

'Well, perhaps you should try hard. Create something for me.'

'For you!'

'Indeed. It would give me great pleasure to help a young scribe along the way.'

'I am flattered, honoured that you should make such an offer, but I assure you I am not that good.'

'Let me be the judge of that. You have ideas for stories?'

'Well, yes. Ideas I have.'

'Come back to my apartment for a late-night cocktail, and you can tell me about your ideas. Perhaps I can help you—help you focus.'

For a moment, Daniel seemed on the verge of refusing, and then gently, he leaned forward and placed a hand on De Lacy's sleeve. 'I'd love to,' he said, almost in a whisper.

Chapter Six

The first meeting of The Murder Club took place in February 1919 in a private dining room at the Garrick Club. The theatricality of the establishment filled with memorabilia of the great eighteenth-century actor-manager, David Garrick, suited Ambrose De Lacy's humour. The Murder Club was entirely his idea, and he had chosen the six other members with care. They were clever, successful writers but neither as clever nor as successful as he. When someone had suggested that Arthur Conan Doyle should be invited to join, De Lacy had rejected the idea with some force. The Sherlock man was far too prominent an author; De Lacy knew he would be too easily overshadowed in such illustrious company.

On that cold, damp, and foggy night at the Garrick, the members of the newly formed association held their first dinner. It was a lively occasion, the writers unleashed from their lonely rooms where they carried out their solitary profession, mingling solely with fictitious characters of their own creation and arranging a murder or two, were like prisoners released from their cells eager to talk and engage with real people, especially those of a similar occupation.

De Lacy sat back and viewed the scene rather like a scientist peering through a microscope at an intriguing group of microbes. There were three men and three women chatting in a relaxed yet strangely animated fashion. Immediately on his right was Vivien Dowson, stout, plump-faced, fiftyish, dressed, De Lacy thought, like a man in a heavy tweed outfit and sporting a collar and tie. A pair of heavy dark spectacles hung on the end of her nose. Her grey hair was cut short in a masculine manner, and her voice had a deep guttural sound. Despite her rather imposing appearance, De Lacy found her an amusing woman who made no attempt to hide her lesbian leanings. She wrote cunning 'whodunnits' featuring an elderly spinster, which had caught the imagination of the public. Dowson had been a nurse in her youth, and she often used her medical knowledge, particularly that of poisons, in her mysteries. De Lacy envied her clever and precise plotting but thought her books lacked drama and suspense.

Next to her was Meg Granger. She was the youngest of the company. She had not yet reached the age of thirty but had recently penned a successful whodunnit written during a lengthy convalescence rumoured to be tuberculosis from which, De Lacy observed, she seemed to have made a full recovery. The book was like its author, well-formed and sensuous, but De Lacy found that she was a little unpredictable at times as though she was not always fully in control of her emotions. That is why her writing was so effective. It had been Granger's publisher who had approached De Lacy, pushing hard for her to be admitted to the Club. 'This is a girl who is going to be big,' he said. 'She will be an asset to your group. She is young and fresh.' De Lacy had seen the sense of this notion, and so had agreed.

Meg Granger was not a pretty woman, but she oozed sex appeal and attractiveness. De Lacy imagined her as a glamorous spider and woe betide any man who was lured on to her web.

The other female in the group was Briony Lodge, an Australian with a rather overwhelming, spirited character. She was tall and lean with a gentle Australian accent and a high opinion of herself and her writings. Her novels featured a detective agency based in a small town in the Australian bush. The stories were full of local colour and, as such, brought a touch of the faraway to the world of British mystery fiction. However, De Lacy had been very apprehensive about inviting her in the first place, but his agent had recommended that he did so. 'She is a force to be reckoned with,' he had been told. 'Better have her inside the pen rather than outside causing mischief.' De Lacy saw the sense of this observation: mischief is the last thing he wanted. As he had got to know her a little better, he could see that failing to invite her to be a member of the club would have been regarded by her as a rebuttal and would no doubt prompt her to cause problems. She was a woman of strong opinions and had no restraint in expressing them. De Lacy thought it best not to contradict or antagonise this Australian firebrand, with her highly charged emotions. It was the best policy for a quiet life.

At the far end of the table was Jacob Brown. Nearing sixty years of age, he was the oldest of the members. He was a fat, red-faced man with a bulbous nose and bulging, bloodshot eyes. He wore an old brown three-piece corduroy suit, the jacket of which was covered in grey flakes of tobacco from the numerous cigarettes he smoked. De Lacy referred to Brown in private as 'Farmer Brown' partly because he owned a smallholding in the Cotswolds and partly because his detective stories were always set in the countryside featuring agricultural folk, farmers, yokels, and the lord of the manor who was either the villain or the victim. De Lacy regarded his books as predictable potboilers, but they had cornered a comfortable niche in the market.

Then there was Lord Carfax, a sleek skeleton in a dinner suit. Anthony Carfax was in possession of those characteristically smooth polished features with high cheekbones and expressionless eyes innate in the aristocratic breed, indicative of the fact that they have never really had to deal with the usual stresses and strains meted out to the bulk of humanity. Money cushioned them from all those inconvenient trials and tribulations of the weary workaday world. It was true that it seemed that Carfax had no need to raise a finger in any pursuit resembling work for the rest of his pampered life, save when he was raising a wine glass to his lips. However, for some reason, he had taken it upon himself to try his hand at writing mystery stories and found not only that he was reasonably adept at this, but he had also been successful in building up a burgeoning readership. His character was Captain Devonshire, whom some perceived was a thinly disguised alter ego of the author himself, complete with Carfax's finely curled moustache. Devonshire was a dashing cavalry officer who wooed the ladies and donned a burglar's mask by night relieving the wealthy of their precious baubles. The notion of a gentleman crook had caught the public's imagination, and the books were growing in popularity. De Lacy despised Carfax intensely, and he was not alone in this. His Lordship was generally disliked by his fellow scribes merely on the grounds that everything seemed to come so easily to him, money, possessions, and the ability to knock off a bestseller without breaking a sweat.

Despite De Lacy's virulent dislike of Carfax, he had reasoned that his notoriety and society connections may well be a real asset to the club and so with gritted teeth, he had invited him to join.

'Delighted, old boy,' Carfax had replied with a broad grisly smile which exposed a row of uneven teeth. 'Happy to join any group for a slap-up meal with plenty of the old grape juice.'

The remaining member of the club was Professor Alan Watkins, who wrote under the pseudonym of Adam Worth. He penned historical mystery stories featuring Father Charles, a peripatetic monk from the sixteenth century. These stories were rich in medieval detail, his particular academic discipline. Watkins was a young man of thirty-five who wore his fame and academic qualifications lightly. He had a square, handsome face tipped by short curly hair, and his light voice was tinged with an accent that betrayed his Welsh roots. He was, in De Lacy's eyes, 'a harmless, pleasant enough fellow' and no real threat to the others in the club. He could not see the meanderings of a loquacious wandering monk who was constantly spouting about the medical properties of herbs found in the hedgerows and meadows and the finer details of ancient charters overtaking the sales of others in the club and in particular, his own novels featuring his current detective hero, Inspector Curzon.

De Lacy sat back in his chair and took a sip of wine as he surveyed all the members of his club and smiled. His club. He was the master magician who had brought them all together.

Once the meal had concluded and the waiting staff had removed all the dishes and brought in a large decanter of brandy with glasses, Ambrose De Lacy rose from his chair and tapped his glass with a pen.

'Ladies and Gentlemen,' he began imperiously, 'fellow members of The Murder Club, I welcome you with bloodstained hands, a smoking revolver, and a phial of cyanide to the first meeting of this illustrious group.'

This announcement was followed by a gentle laughter and a ripple of applause.

'Well done, sir, brilliant idea,' stated Lord Carfax raising his glass in tribute.

De Lacy gave a nod of acknowledgement before continuing. 'As you all know, the topic for discussion tonight is Modus Operandi—what methods we use to kill off our victims. Who, I wonder, can come up with the most ingenious way to commit murder? Who will be the first to start?'

Chapter Seven

While Wilde listened with interest as De Lacy described the members of the Murder Club, Kishen was busy making notes for future reference. When De Lacy had finished his recital, Wilde's blue eyes flashed with interest; he stubbed out his cigarette and remained silent for some moments, his mind digesting the information that had just been presented to him.

'If you had to choose from this illustrious company one who would take it into their head to murder you, who would you choose?'

De Lacy seemed shocked at this query. "Gracious, what a suggestion. These are all colleagues, respectable fellows.'

'Oh, believe me, many murderers are respectable fellows.'

De Lacy seemed disgruntled at this response. 'I wasn't being serious when I suggested that one of the members of the club could be the person who sent that accursed letter... the devil who is planning to kill me.'

Wilde raised a sardonic eyebrow. 'And yet, when prompted, they were the only people you could think of who may harbour sufficient animosity towards you to carry out the deed.'

'Well, yes...but...not seriously. The culprit could easily be a stranger, some mentally disturbed reader....'

Wilde shook his head. 'May I redirect your attention to the wording of the note: 'you don't *deserve* to live.' This is a very personal statement and points to someone who knows you, someone who, rightly or wrongly, is convinced you have done them, or someone they know some serious harm. So, I ask you again, is there anyone that you can think of who bears such a grudge?'

De Lacy ran his hand across his forehead, a look of apprehension on his features. 'As I told you before,' he said at length, 'no.'

Wilde did not believe him but did not pursue the matter.

'So, Mr De Lacy, we are left with the members of your Murder Club. Let me press you further to choose one who you believe has the potential to be your murderer.'

The author shook his head vigorously. 'I have no idea. It is impossible to choose. No one has shown open animosity towards me, although I am sure most, if not all, would be happy if I were no longer writing books, providing such strong opposition. However, if one of them was intending to snuff me out—why now? The Club has been in existence for just over three years....'

'And in those three years, your reputation and success as a crime novelist has grown even more, has it not?'

At this observation, De Lacy could not help but deliver a dark satisfied grin. 'I suppose so,' he said, attempting modesty but failing.

'Unless you can come up with any more potential candidates for the role of your would-be assassin, then I suggest we start with the Murder Club.'

'It seems that you are grasping at straws....'

'When one is presented with only straws—what else does one grasp? When do you hold your next meeting?'

'One is arranged for next week.'

'Is it possible for myself and Kishen to attend?'

De Lacy cast a wary glance at Kishen. 'Your assistant?'

'Kishen is my associate, not my assistant. We work as a team.' Wilde leaned forward in his chair for emphasis. 'We come as a package if we come at all.'

There was an awkward pause which hung in the air until the author deigned to respond. 'Very well,' said De Lacy with some reluctance.

'Good. It will give us a chance to observe and chat with your members, see if we can pick up any clues, any nuances which will help in determining if one of them is the guilty party.'

'The dinner is at the Garrick at eight o'clock next Wednesday. If you are to attend, it would be best in order to explain your presence if you will take on the role of guest speaker. Could you give a short talk concerning your experiences as a private detective?'

Wilde nodded. 'I suppose so. I am sure I can come up with something. In the meantime, let me know if you have further correspondence from your well-wisher and if you can think of any other individual who thinks you 'deserve' to die.'

'And what do you make of all that, Rupert?' asked Kishen with a mischievous grin after their visitor had departed.

'Well, old lad, I am convinced there is more to this matter than Ambrose De Lacy is prepared to admit. A fact I rather like.'

'Why so?'

'Because it adds spice to the investigation. It means that we have detective work at both ends of the case: we need to find out the truth concerning our author client and discover who wants to bump the fellow off.' Wilde rubbed his hands with enthusiasm. 'Puzzles to solve, my dear Kishen. Puzzles to solve.'

'Do you really think someone would actually be prepared to bump off Mr De Lacy—as you so delicately phrase it—just because he sells a few more books than others in his field?'

'Stranger things have happened. Who knows what a warped mind may take as a motive for murder? And it ain't a few more books, Kishen old lad; I am sure it's thousands.'

'But there would be no guarantee should our illustrious client no longer be around, that the public would start buying the murderer's novels.'

'Of course not, but then we are back to the warped mind I alluded to. Fellows with a twisted cerebellum do not work with logic. However, I have a strong feeling there is a more personal reason for this hatred of Ambrose. Nothing to do with books at all. Forgive me if I return to that word in the threatening letter, 'deserve.' That word speaks of a deep-seated personal reason for wanting to get rid of Mr De Lacy rather than his burgeoning sales at the bookshop. However, only time will tell.'

'And what will you do in the meantime?'

Wilde smiled and patted Kishen on the arm. 'Ah, my fearless bloodhound,

I'll set you the task of coming up with a detailed biography of Monsieur De Lacy. Let's find out all we can about the fellow.'

'And you?

'I will simply wait for developments. I am fairly certain that I will not have to wait for very long.'

Chapter Eight

Ambrose De Lacy spent the afternoon at his desk trying to work on his latest Inspector Curzon novel. The going was hard. His mind had difficulty concentrating on the perils of his daredevil detective when he was aware that his own life was in danger. He couldn't write himself out of that dark corner. At any slight noise, he would turn abruptly in his chair and scour the room behind him. He was wretched, not feeling secure in his own home.

As evening beckoned and shadows grew, he decided to dine out. He felt he would be safer in a public place rather than at home alone. He made his way to La Locanda, his favourite Italian restaurant less than a mile away from his apartment. Here, seated in his usual corner, with a plate of Pasta Fagioli al Forno, and a bottle of Chianti, he began to relax a little, for the first time since he received that wretched communication. By the end of the meal, when the coffee and cognac had arrived, he was feeling almost merry. He sat back in his chair, the dark clouds of worry having for the moment faded from his horizon with the assistance of food and alcohol. He allowed his mind to wander and whenever it did so, as usual when he was in this lightly intoxicated state, his thoughts inevitably made their way to Daniel. De Lacy's vivid imagination seemed to conjure up an image of the young man seated across from him as though he was a dining companion—there in the flesh.

'Hello, my dear boy,' he addressed this phantom image, his voice catching at the back of his throat. 'How wonderful to see you.' He raised his glass in a toast, tears pricking his eyes. As he sipped the cognac, the image faded.

For some moments, he permitted the sadness to hold him, and then as an escape he allowed his memory to transport him to their first meeting in the Café Royal and then on to what followed: Daniel accompanying him to his apartment. More drinks, cigars, unspoken moments, the tentative glances of passion. He had been too apprehensive—too cowardly—to make the final move. He later learned that Daniel was simply waiting for it to happen. He was never one to take the initiative. De Lacy was now aware that Daniel expected life to come to him. If it didn't, he just moved on.

'Well, I'd better be toddling along,' Daniel said after they had two glasses of champagne. It was obvious to him that the famous author was not going to take things further.

'Yes, yes, of course,' said De Lacy with considerable dismay. He was annoyed at his failure to make a gesture which would suggest his feelings. His nails dug into the palms of his hands as a kind of self-imposed punishment for being so weak, so timid. Why hadn't he been bold enough to take the initiative? Say something, make some subtle indication, or better still, try to kiss the man? What was the worst that could happen? Daniel would knock him down and depart. If suitably appalled, he might beat him to a pulp for his effrontery. So what? It had happened before. But this boy was so beautiful, he didn't want to offend him with his sordid desires if he were not in tune with them also.

Daniel picked up his coat, hat, and cane and moved to the door.

'I say,' cried De Lacy, his voice emerging strangely from a dry throat. 'I have tickets for *Choo Chin Chow* at Her Majesty's tomorrow night. I don't suppose you'd care to join me? We could take supper afterwards.'

Daniel turned and stared at him, and there was an awkward silence. And then that handsome face broke into a broad grin. 'Oh, Ambrose, I'd love to. Heard such good things about the show, and to go there with you, would be the icing on the cake.'

And so, it started.

During the course of the show, it was actually Daniel who made the first gesture. He moved his hand gently in the dark and took hold of De Lacy's. No words were uttered, but the tentative squeeze he gave spoke volumes to the author. The notion of going for a meal after the performance was abandoned, and they headed back to De Lacy's apartment. Within a short time, they were in bed together, making love. To De Lacy, it was wonderful and natural while at the same time miraculous. Miraculous that this young god should show passion and tenderness to him.

Afterwards, as they lay in bed together in the softly lighted room, De Lacy could not resist raising the question. 'What are you doing here with me, Daniel? You could have your choice of any young man. I am twice your age and certainly no oil painting.' He smiled sadly at his own self-deprecation.

Daniel leaned across and kissed De Lacy on the cheek. 'Beauty is in the eye of the beholder, don't you know? Simply, my dear Ambrose, I find you a fascinating creature with a bright inner flame, a flame to which like some helpless butterfly I am irresistibly drawn.'

De Lacy was not enamoured with the analogy—butterflies are often consumed in the flames they are drawn to—but Daniel's sentiments thrilled him.

'How about some champagne to celebrate our tryst, eh?' cried Daniel, leaping out of bed and slipping on a bathrobe that De Lacy had given him.

De Lacy beamed and gave a bright laugh. 'Champers it is, my dear boy.'

Ambrose De Lacy took another sip of his brandy as he recalled that fateful evening once more. For a moment, the memory brought a fleeting smile to his lips, but then it faded. There was always joy at the beginning, he told himself, when the new avenue with enticing golden hopes lay before you. That night was such a beginning, and perhaps it was the happiest time in his relationship with his 'dear boy.' Neither had any idea of the darkness that was waiting just around the corner. For a week, the two men were inseparable, with De Lacy trying as much as possible to ignore the brutal fact that Daniel was soon to be whisked away into the army, training to be an officer, and then hurled onto the battlefields of France. Once there, he may never return.

And then one day, Daniel turned up unexpectedly at Ambrose's flat. He appeared to be in a state of some distress. His hair was askew, and his pale features were glistening with a fine sheen of perspiration. There was also the appearance of a blossoming bruise on his cheek. De Lacy was shocked and distressed to see his lover in such a state. He led him to the chaise longue and poured him a large brandy.

'What on earth has happened?' he asked, stroking Daniel's hair.

The youth burst into tears. 'I am so ashamed,' he cried, the words emerging through shuddering sobs.

'Ashamed? About what?'

Daniel shook his head in a gesture of despair.

'Come on, my dear,' said De Lacy, sitting down by him and placing his arm around the young man's shoulders. 'You must tell me. You have to tell me.'

Daniel took a large gulp of brandy before replying. 'I've been a fool,' he said, his voice strained with emotion. 'A giant idiot.'

De Lacy said nothing, waiting for more information. It pained him to see Daniel in this disturbing state of distress.

'I...I owe money. A lot of money to... a set of powerful men. And they want it.'

'I don't understand. How do you owe this money?'

'Gambling. I gamble to live, Ambrose. And that means I take risks... get involved with unscrupulous people at times. Bad company. I take risks and play for high stakes with money I don't have. You see, I lied to you about my allowance. It has all gone. I am virtually penniless.'

De Lacy shook his head. He could hardly believe what he was hearing. 'What on earth are you saying?' he asked, although with his writer's mind, he really had more than an inkling of what Daniel was implying.

'I made a foolish wager. High stakes. And lost. Now I owe these men a lot of money, and they have given me three days to come up with the goods—or else.'

'Or else?'

Daniel nodded. 'I fear for my life. They gave me a roughing up as a warning, as an indication of worse things in store if I don't come up with the cash.'

De Lacy jumped to his feet and began pacing the room. 'Why this is terrible. Awful. You must go to the police.'

'No! No, that would be the worst thing I could do. They would kill me for sure if I did that.'

'Kill you!' De Lacy felt a shiver of fear run up his spine. This melodrama was like something out of one of his own thrillers rather than reality. 'Do you...do you really mean that? They would... kill you?"

'Yes.' The reply was a strained whisper. 'I'm afraid that there is only one way of getting these fiends off my back, and that is...to pay them. But I can't. I don't have the money.'

For some moments, there was silence in the room, and then De Lacy said, 'How much do you owe?'

There was another brief silence before Daniel replied. 'Five hundred pounds.'

'What!'

'I know, I know. It's a crazy amount. I have been an utter fool. I don't know what to do.' He began crying again.

De Lacy gave a weary shrug and sat down again by Daniel. 'Calm yourself, dear boy,' he said gently, putting his arm around the young man again and stroking his hair as though he were a distressed child. 'There is only one solution, my dear. I will give you the money.'

'Oh, I couldn't....'

'What is the alternative? I don't want to be visiting you on a mortuary slab in the near future. The only way to ensure your safety is to pay.'

'But I can't....'

'There is no other option, is there? You are unable to pay them yourself; the alternative is unthinkable. Daniel, you must know that I care for you dearly, and if five hundred pounds ensures your safety, it is a small price to pay. But promise me this: you won't gamble or mix with these people again.'

'Of course.' Daniel threw his arm around De Lacy and kissed him on the cheek. 'God bless you,' he said, the voice croaky with emotion. De Lacy responded with another kiss, on the lips this time.

Half an hour later, Daniel left De Lacy's flat with a cheque safely secured in his jacket pocket. As he reached the lift, he punched the air with a fist, a wide grin illuminating his features.

CHAPTER EIGHT

That night Bolly received a phone call: 'The game has started. Bullseye for the first move.'

Chapter Nine

Now De Lacy grew even closer to Daniel, inviting him to dine with him most evenings and also enticing him into his bed. He bought the young man presents, including a gold watch which was inscribed 'To Daniel, my sweet love, Ambrose.' The author believed that he had really found his soul mate and was the happiest he had ever been in his life.

One sunny afternoon, as they strolled in St James's Park, Ambrose found the courage to raise the subject. 'Must you go? Into the army, I mean?'

'What else can I do? I'm signed up. I can't avoid the issue. They'll only come after me and then I could be demoted to Private or worse - incarcerated for attempting to dodge the draft. That would be charming.'

'I know I'm being selfish, but I don't want to lose you—not just when we've just begun.'

Daniel gave De Lacy's arm a squeeze. 'I know, Ambrose. Don't you think I feel the same way? And I know what you're thinking. I'll be off to France, and you'll never see me again. I'll be blown up by some German mortar bomb or caught by a sniper's bullet. I'll be like that poet fellow, lying in the corner of some foreign field.'

De Lacy screwed his eyes up tight. 'Don't, don't, for God's sake.'

Daniel gave a heavy sigh. 'Sorry, but it's what you're thinking, ain't it?'

'Of course, it is.'

'Well, I can't promise not to get shot or blown up, but as I've told you, I do believe I lead a charmed life, and I'll be bouncing back to old Blighty when the war is over.'

'But that could be years from now.'

With this truism, the pair fell into silence.

As they approached the park gates, Daniel gave a little skip and swung his cane in a theatrical fashion. 'Come on, let's get a drink, eh? Cheer ourselves. Begone dull care! It's pointless being miserable when we do have time together.'

'Of course.' Ambrose De Lacy smiled; his features warmed, but his heart was leaden.

They found a smart bar nearby and ordered champagne. After a few glasses, both men felt more cheerful: the bubbles helping them to recover their own buoyancy.

'When do you actually have to report for this blasted training business?' De Lacy asked.

'By the end of the month.' It was a lie, but a smooth one. By now, untruths tripped easily from Daniel's tongue. He was never going to put on a rough army uniform and be shunted off to France to take part in this irritating war. He was not prepared to take the same dangerous route as his brother. That is why he had bribed a desperate down and out with consumption to take his place at the medical examination. Now his name was firmly fixed in the list of those excused from compulsory conscription. He was a free man, a free man on his way to a fortune.

'By the end of the month. Gracious, that's just over a week away.'

Daniel stared into his glass. 'I know.'

'This bloody war,' snarled De Lacy. And then a thought struck him. 'Daniel, as you said, we must make the best of the time left to us. I know of a little bolt hole well away from London which I've used on occasion when I've had a challenging book to deal with. It's in Cornwall. The quiet and isolation with none of the usual interruptions helps me tremendously to sort out the tricky plot details. An an ideal place for privacy and seclusion. Clean country air, the sea, and solitude. Why don't we go down there for a long weekend? Create a wonderful memory to sustain us during the period of separation.'

Daniel did not respond immediately to this suggestion. At length, he smiled and touched De Lacy's sleeve. 'It sounds wonderful... but it could be painful, allowing us so much intimate time together before the brutal rift. I don't know.'

De Lacy, now enthused with the idea, waved his hands airily as though brushing Daniel's reservations away. 'Nonsense, we will have a wonderful time. We'll be able to really get to know each other without any distractions—just three days—and nights—of you and me.' He reached out and grabbed Daniel's sleeve. 'We must do it.'

Daniel gave a gentle shrug of the shoulders. 'If you are sure....'

'Of course, I am, my dear boy. It will be wonderful.'

'Very well. Cornwall, it is.'

De Lacy gave a guffaw of pleasure and raised his glass. 'To Cornwall.'

To Cornwall, thought Daniel, and the end of this turgid affair.

Bolly received a telephone call late that evening.

The voice at the other end said: 'The curtain is about to fall, and the treasure chest is about to open. Let me tell you about it.'

Chapter Ten

Kishen sat in the outer office of the managing director of Arnold & Son, publishers. He was perched awkwardly on a wooden chair, knees clenched together, his hat held tightly in his hands, and a thin sheen of perspiration on his forehead. He was feeling nervous. He had not done this kind of thing before. In previous investigations with Rupert, he had merely assisted his friend and not been sent on a mission on his own to pretend to be someone else. As a Hindu, he was ill-equipped for deception and impersonation. It required consummate acting skills, which he was fairly certain he did not possess.

He gazed across the room at the secretary who was busy typing, the clacking of the keys like little hammers banging in his head. He was suddenly taken with the idea of rising from the chair, making some mumbled excuse, and leaving. As this notion grew in intent, the intercom buzzed on the secretary's desk. She ceased typing and glanced across at Kishen.

'Mr Arnold Junior will see you now,' she said and nodded to the door to her left.

Kishen nodded, managing a nervous smile before walking stiffly towards the rear office.

'Come, come in, Mr Chabra, and take a seat.' Mr Arnold Junior was, to Kishen's surprise, a solidly built man who appeared to be somewhere in his fifties, if his thinning grey hair and lined features were any guide. Kishen had assumed that the word junior indicated a young man. He wondered how old Mr Arnold Senior would be—if he were still alive.

'Got your memo here, which says you are the British correspondent of

Mystery and Mayhem, an Indian magazine, and you are writing a piece about our best-selling author Ambrose De Lacy whose sales in India are beginning to take off. So, you reckon your piece will help boost our Ambrose in your country, do you?'

'That… that is the intention.'

'Well, that is good news for us. How can I help?'

'I am wanting to write a personal profile about Mr De Lacy. Our readers, who enjoy his books immensely, want to know all about the great man—what makes him tick.'

Arnold junior pursed his lips. 'Wouldn't you be better talking to the man himself? I am just his publisher; we have merely a business relationship.'

'Oh, I am intending to talk to Mr De Lacy, indeed. But such interviews often produce very subjective views.' Kishen paused and grinned awkwardly. 'We are only told what the subject wishes us to know.'

'Oh, I see. You're after secrets then.' The publisher's face clouded with suspicion.

'No, no. Nothing unseemly, I assure you. Just details which will help to give me the material to produce a rounded picture of this eminent author.'

'Can you assure me of that? I don't want to be involved in anything which would prove detrimental to Mr De Lacy or this publishing house.'

'Certainly, sir. We are a respectable periodical, but I am sure there are many fascinating respectable aspects to Mr De Lacy which would interest and intrigue our readers and, of course, prompt them to purchase his books.' Kishen flashed a reassuring smile to add weight to this statement. Slowly, he was gaining confidence, and to his surprise, he was beginning to enjoy his assumed role. Perhaps he had a talent for this kind of subterfuge, after all.

'Fair enough,' said Arnold. 'However, I'm not really in a position to help you myself. As I indicated, I only know Mr De Lacy on a formal business level. I offer him a contract, he signs it, he writes a book, and we sell it. As such, I know very little of Mr De Lacy's character, likes, dislikes, or even how he manages to conjure up such fascinating and popular novels.'

'Oh dear.' *And things were going so well.*

'What I suggest is that you have a word with Miss Prothero. Jennifer

Prothero, she is Mr De Lacy's editor and works very closely with him on the final manuscript. She will have more to tell you about him than I.'

And so it was that Kishen was ushered into a small office on the lower floor to be introduced to Miss Jennifer Prothero, a thin, stick-like middle-aged woman with greying hair tied tightly into a bun. A pair of golden pince-nez was balanced on a large, crooked nose. She looked up from her desk and gazed with a piercing stare at Kishen as he was introduced to her by Arnold Junior, who explained the purpose of his visit.

'I've never heard of your publication,' observed Miss Prothero tartly.

'Really. I am surprised,' Kishen volleyed back.

'So, what do you wish to know about old Ambrose?'

Kishen shrugged casually. 'Just your impression of this valued author. How does he create his stories? Does he have many friends? What are his interests? Things like that.'

'Huh, tittle-tattle, you mean.'

'Maybe. Things you would not find in any official biography. I wish to make Mr De Lacy fascinating, intriguing, to delve into some of his own mysteries.'

Miss Prothero gave a harsh laugh. 'Let it be established at the outset that anything I say about old Ambrose is not to be attributed directly to me or this publishing house. Is that understood?'

'Certainly. As you wish. Tell me, why do you call him old Ambrose? He is only in his forties.'

'It's because he's a bit of an old woman.' Miss Prothero chuckled. 'So fussy, so pedantic, like an old maid. Still, I suppose that comes with the territory.'

'What do you mean?'

'You've met him, haven't you?'

Kishen was puzzled. 'I'm sorry....'

'Call yourself a journalist! You could not describe old Ambrose as a man's man, could you...? Or, I suppose, in one way, you could.'

The veil was lifted for Kishen. 'Oh, I see.'

Miss Prothero placed a finger to her lips. 'That must never be breathed abroad. Understand?'

Kishen nodded.

'What I can tell you which is fit for public consumption is that Ambrose De Lacy has a remarkable brain. He has the greatest facility for coming up with clever plots for his novels. He never seems to struggle to concoct a thrilling scenario. It is a gift. I deal with a lot of writers, and there is no one like De Lacy for churning out material of such superb quality. He works like clockwork, and never once has he been late for a deadline. This, of course, makes my job a lot easier, so I'm always happy when a new De Lacy manuscript lands on my desk. As a person, he is very much a private individual. Keeps himself to himself. After working with him for nearly ten years, I know no more about his private life than I did when I was first introduced to him.'

'What about his friends?'

'Indeed, what about his friends? I know of none. Of course, he knows a number of writers in the same genre, and there are those authors in his Murder Club, but really as far as I can judge, these are just acquaintances, not really close friends. No doubt he may have had some 'romantic' dalliances, but I know nothing of these, nor do I want to. That's about it, sonny. If I were you, I'd choose a different subject for your article. There is nothing much to say about Mr Ambrose De Lacy other than he is a brilliant writer. However, he is a somewhat cold and solitary fish; his personal and private life is a closed book. So, there you have it.'

Miss Prothero adjusted her pince-nez and turned her attention back to the sheaf of papers on her desk. It appeared the interview was over. Kishen uttered a gentle thank you and left the room.

Rupert Wilde sat quietly, his eyes closed and his long fingers steepled as he listened intently to Kishen's detailed report regarding his visit to the publishers. When Kishen had finished, Wilde remained silent, his blue eyes hooded in thought for a time before responding.

'I'm afraid it was not a very useful excursion,' observed Kishen.

'I'm not so sure. It certainly strengthens the portrait we have of our client.

And there was this suggestion that De Lacy is homosexual which does not come as a complete surprise, but it certainly opens other avenues.'

'I suppose.'

'I encountered such groups of men at university,' said Wilde.

'Ah.'

'Yes. The N boys, they called themselves. They tried to keep their alliance secret, but it is difficult to keep anything completely under wraps at university.'

'The N Boys?'

'Short for Nancy Boys. The slang term for men of that persuasion. Exposure makes them an easy target for blackmail. The penalties for homosexual practices are severe. It would certainly destroy De Lacy's reputation and livelihood if the truth was made public.'

'Blackmail? Do you think this may have implications in the De Lacy investigation?'

'Not sure, but it does confirm my suspicions that there is more to this case than we were led to believe. De Lacy denied that there was anyone who bore him a deep personal grudge. Maybe that was because he did not want to reveal anything about his personal love life.'

'If that is the case,' observed Kishen, 'he was being a little naïve in consulting a private detective.'

Wilde smiled. 'You would think so. Naïve maybe or convinced that the threat had nothing to do with that side of his life. We need to dig a little deeper.'

Chapter Eleven

The angry heaving waves crashed onto the rocks below the cottage, and the wind howled and beat against the windows, but Ambrose De Lacy was oblivious to the sounds; he was, in fact, oblivious to everything but the words that had just been spoken to him. Words that had pierced his soul and set his mind in turmoil. He stared at his companion, eyes wide with horror and a mouth so dry, and his mind so numbed that for some time, he could not speak.

Eventually, he managed a brief utterance: 'Surely you... are not serious,' he croaked.

''Fraid so,' said his companion nonchalantly, taking a puff on his cigarette. 'You've been fooled, old fellow. Despite your acumen as a mystery writer, you have failed to spot all the clues. You have been so wrapped up in your own self-obsessed fantasy that you could not see the truth right in front of your eyes. It was all a charade. You really believed that I cared about you, loved you.' He allowed himself a theatrical laugh. 'I was convincing, wasn't I?'

'But why?' The words escaped from a very dry throat. De Lacy felt ill and weak. Daniel's demands had knocked the stuffing out of him.

'Money, old boy. Just money. No passion, just greed. It is simply a case of pay up or be damned. I have your letters, very tasty amorous letters, and other pieces of evidence—the watch, for instance, with such a touching inscription—to give credence to my claim. A package to one of the scurrilous newspapers and your reputation and career would be consumed in the flames. Oh, what would the world think if it was revealed that the most famous of authors, one who writes of dark deeds, blood, and murder, was, in fact a homo. A friend of dear Oscar Wilde. And remember what happened to him.'

'You black-hearted scoundrel.'

'Oh, yes, I am a scoundrel. And proud of it. It is only scoundrels who survive in this naughty world.'

There was a long pause before De Lacy responded. 'You fooled me....'

The man gave a cool, sarcastic smile. 'It is more likely that you fooled yourself. We both play act, assume roles, we secret creatures of nature. Nothing is quite real, quite true in our world. We deceive and obfuscate as a form of self-preservation against society and the law. And, of course, the weakness of self-delusion comes at a price. You once gave me five hundred pounds....'

'To help you, yes.'

'Indeed, it did help me. But not in the way you imagine. I am sorry to tell you there were no thugs on my tail demanding payments for gambling debts, just a few trivial bills that needed paying in order for me to maintain my comfortable lifestyle. It was all a charade, old boy. Now I'm after a final payment. It is just a mere five thousand pounds. A small amount to preserve your public persona—to prevent me from whipping off your mask and revealing to the world what kind of man you really are.'

Suddenly the flame of anger ignited within De Lacy's breast, and with clenched fists, he took a step further towards his companion.

'Whoa,' said Daniel, in no way intimidated by De Lacy's threatening manner. 'Don't go all melodramatic on me. Attempting to knock me down will not change anything apart from degrading you. And haven't you degraded yourself enough already?'

'You heartless unprincipled bastard!' De Lacy, at last, found his voice, and the utterance echoed loudly around the room.

'Of course, I cannot deny that. In the abusive metaphorical sense, of course. I can assure you that I was born on the right side of the blanket.'

Ambrose De Lacy suddenly felt weak, his body finally reacting and absorbing the news and the threat he had just received. The anger and the shock consumed him. His legs gave way, and he sank down into a chair.

'Looks like you could do with a drink, old man,' said his companion, cheerily. 'And then we can talk about the money, the very large amount of money, you are about to pay me...for my silence. And to help me disappear.'

Chapter Twelve

A few evenings later, following De Lacy's visit to see Rupert Wilde, the author was just about to finish his writing duties for the day. He wrote mainly in the mornings when his brain was fresh and again late at night when alcohol had fired his imagination, and he could add felicitous inventive touches to his earlier endeavours. He was rarely stuck for ideas, plot developments, or the creation of exciting twists in the narrative. He gazed over the last page and was pleased with the result. Just as he was about to place the new sheets into a folder, the doorbell rang. His heart skipped a beat. He glanced at the clock on the mantelshelf. Eleven thirty. Who on earth could be calling at this time of night?

The bell rang again. Should he answer the door? What if it was the author of the threatening letter here to carry out the dreadful deed on his own doorstep? Another ring. By God, the fellow was insistent. Cautiously he moved from his office into the sitting room and picked up a poker from the hearth on the way.

He moved down the narrow hallway, unlocked the door, and opened it a few inches with great apprehension before peering out. There was the face of Anthony Carfax staring back at him. He had an idiotic grin on his face, which informed De Lacy that the man was inebriated. He had seen Carfax wear the same rather stupefied visage previously, when he had been heavily in drink.

'What the hell do you want at this time of night?' snapped De Lacy. His dark concerns fading.

'A little word, old boy. A little word and a bit of a crutch. Can I come in?'

came the reply.

With some reluctance, De Lacy opened the door wide and bade the man enter. He walked ahead of him into the sitting room, slipping the poker back in place. 'Let's make this short, Anthony. It is late, and I'm rather tired,' he said brusquely.

'Yes, yes, of course. But aren't you going to offer your guest a drink?'

'I would have thought you'd had enough already.'

Carfax gave an amused gurgle. 'You can never have too much, old boy. Keeps the darkness of the world at bay.'

'Whisky suit you?' De Lacy asked with some reservation.

'Fine, fine.'

He supplied his visitor with a drink. 'Now, what's this all about?'

'Cheers,' said Carfax downing the shot of whisky in one gulp. 'Well, it's like this, Ambrose, I'm in a bit of a hole.'

'No doubt it is one you've dug yourself.'

Carfax nodded. 'Indeed. With a damned great shovel. I'm up to my eyes in it, barely peeping over the top.' He gave a bleak chuckle.

'Debt?'

Another nod. 'I'm afraid my neck is on the line. I need a couple of hundred pretty damned quick. A gentleman must pay his debts if a gentleman is desirous of avoiding bodily harm or having his name dragged in the mud.'

'Why come to me, Carfax? Extract the amount required from your own coffers.'

'If only I could, but I'm afraid the cupboard is bare. I have to admit I have been somewhat careless, somewhat profligate.' Another bleak chuckle. 'My inheritance has somehow evaporated. Gone with the wind. It's very costly being a peer of the realm, you know, keeping a large townhouse and a staff of servants. I'm not you, you know, a fabulously wealthy author whose every book makes a mint. I'm lucky if my royalties buy me dinner at the Ritz. I am not half as successful as people think. What makes things worse, I have a feeling that my publishers are considering giving me the great heave-ho. Last book was a bit of a stinker, I'm afraid.'

This was news to Ambrose. Carfax's first crime novel had been a great success and had attracted much attention. At first, De Lacy thought he had a serious rival, but his Lordship hadn't been able to repeat his initial success with subsequent novels. He was a dilettante writer not prepared to put in the hours and effort required to create effective fiction. The lure of the drinking and gambling clubs was too great for him. De Lacy had always assumed that his Lordship's inherited wealth was a cushion to any of his reckless activities. It seemed not. The fool appeared to have frittered it away. The golden egg was smashed.

'Just a couple hundred pounds...', said Carfax, leaning forward and clutching De Lacy's sleeve. 'Not a king's ransom, is it?'

'And how much next time, eh? You are a fool, Carfax, and an incompetent one at that. I am not in the habit of throwing money—my hard-earned money—down the drain. The answer is no.'

'A hundred then...'

'It is past my bedtime. I really would like you to go now.'

'You...you won't help me?' There was a note of incredulity in his voice.

'Correct.'

Carfax's features darkened, surprise giving way to anger, the eyes suddenly blazing with vitriolic malice. 'You... you bastard... you...' Words failed him, so he threw his whisky glass at the marble hearth, where it shattered into tiny crystal fragments.

'You know the way out,' De Lacy said calmly.

Carfax turned swiftly and made his way with uncertain strides to the door. Before leaving, he swung round to face De Lacy once more. 'You bastard,' he said again, but this time there was no fury in his voice. It was low and sinister. 'You're a slimy heartless... I could kill you for this!'

These words stabbed De Lacy in the heart. They were an open threat. With a sneer, Carfax left, slamming the door behind him.

De Lacy leapt forward and locked the door hurriedly. With his heart pounding, he returned to the sitting room, the words 'I could kill you' drumming in his brain. Was Carfax the demon who had sent that accursed threatening letter? Did he mean to kill him? He slumped down on the sofa and placed his head in his hands. He would have to tell Wilde about this in the morning.

Eventually, he rose and, switching off the two table lamps which gave soft illumination to the room, he made his way to his bedroom, although he harboured little hope in his mind that he would get much sleep tonight. Then, in the gloom, he heard a noise. It was one that he recognised. It was the flap of the letter box.

He made his way down the hall, clicking on the light as he did so. He froze in horror to see a long foolscap envelope lying on the mat. It looked identical to the one that had contained the threatening note. The envelope simply bore his name in capital letters in the familiar purple ink.

He stared at the envelope for some time before raising sufficient courage to pick it up. With shaking hands, he tore it open and extracted a sheet of note paper. It bore four words printed in capital letters:

REMEMBERING DANIEL AND ROSEMULLION

Ambrose De Lacy uttered a strangled cry, halfway between a moan and a muted scream. His body shook with fear as though it was attacked by a sudden fever.

His eyes transfixed by the message, he cried out, 'No, no!'

As the sound of this shriek of despair faded, he screwed up the letter and envelope in one violent, dramatic action and then rushed into the sitting room and threw them into the wastepaper bin. In his disturbed state of mind, this action was erasing their presence from his life. He had never received that cursed message, and he would wipe it from his memory.

Otherwise, he would go mad.

The mysterious letter-sender, whom we shall call the stranger, had observed Lord Carfax's visit to De Lacy's apartment. In fact, it had delayed them from delivering their latest missive. The stranger didn't want it to arrive while the author had someone with him. They had recognised his Lordship and knew who he was and of his membership in the Murder Club. The stranger knew that the two men were not exactly good friends and was somewhat puzzled and intrigued by this late-night call. Standing close to the door, the stranger overheard Carfax's angry tones and the words of his threat, 'I could kill you for this!' That phrase sparked an idea in the stranger's brain.

In another part of the city, Rupert Wilde was sitting up in bed, reading. He was just coming to the end of *Desire for Murder* by Ambrose De Lacy. He had found it an entertaining experience. He wasn't an avid reader of crime fiction, but he could see that this was an effective and accomplished example of the genre. Ambrose De Lacy was obviously a clever man, a clever man with a corkscrew mind. Wilde had tackled the novel because he believed one could gain a lot of information about an author's character from his writings.

The detached and unemotional side to the author's nature was reflected in his prose, and his characters, very few of whom generated any sympathy with the reader. However, there was a keen intelligence at work in the novel, which, Wilde assumed, was typical of his other stories. It was an intelligence, Wilde mused, that would, in real life, protect De Lacy from openly creating enemies. He would keep his thoughts to himself and make no aggressive gestures to ruffle feathers. Any dislike or hatred he harboured in his bosom would find an outlet in unobtrusive ways. And it was clear to Wilde from his first meeting with the author that he was not prepared to reveal any of his private thoughts, relationships, or proclivities and it was probably in this dark secret region where the solution to the mystery concerning the threatening letter lay. He was not ruling out that the would-be assassin was one of the Murder Club members, but for the moment, that notion seemed a little obvious and somewhat fragile. As he had observed to Kishen, he would have to dig a little deeper, and that would mean a certain subterfuge and sleight of hand. With care, he placed the novel on his bedside table, turned off the lamp, and settled down for a good night's rest.

Chapter Thirteen

'How was the concert last night?' Wilde asked, gazing across the table at his companion, Kishen, who was busy buttering a thin slice of toast. It was breakfast time the following morning, and Wilde was feeling cheerful as a plan connected with the De Lacy case was taking a very pleasing shape in his mind.

"It was quite excellent,' came the reply.

'Tchaikovsky, wasn't it?'

'Mmm,' Kishen muttered, his mouth full of toast. 'The fifth symphony.'

'Very romantic, somewhat sentimental, especially the second movement.'

'Is there anything wrong with that?'

Wilde grinned. 'No, not really. If you like that sort of thing.' He laughed. 'I prefer something a little more rigorous. I'm more of a Beethoven man, I think.' He waved his arms as though conducting an orchestra while humming the opening bars of Beethoven's Fifth.

Before Kishen could respond, the telephone rang.

'I'll get it,' said Wilde moving swiftly to the table which housed the receiver.

'It's Ambrose De Lacy. I need to see you urgently.' The voice was hoarse and tense. 'There have been developments,' he added dramatically.

'Like what?'

'I don't want to discuss details over the telephone.'

'Very well,' said Wilde, checking his watch. 'Can you come over here at ten o'clock?'

'Yes, yes. Goodbye.' The line went dead.

'Well, something has rattled old Ambrose's cage,' Wilde mused, returning to the breakfast table.

'What has happened?' sked Kishen.

'He wouldn't say. Apparently, he didn't want to talk about it over the phone so he's coming round here for ten. Strange, in a way, this fits in very neatly with my plans.'

'Really, in what way?'

'I'll explain later….'

'Oh, it's you playing your cards close to your chest time again is it, leaving Kishen in the dark?'

'I'm not going to leave you in the dark; I will explain all to you later. But, in the meantime, I need to ask you a favour.'

At ten o'clock on the dot, the doorbell rang, and Kishen answered the door. Ambrose De Lacy bustled past him in a brusque manner. On entering the sitting room and finding it empty, he threw down his hat in exasperation. 'Where is he? Where is Mr Wilde?'

'Would you care for a cup of tea, or perhaps you would prefer coffee?' said Kishen.

'Neither. Where is Mr Wilde? I have important information to impart concerning my case.'

'I am afraid Mr Wilde is not here at the moment. He has had to go out on an urgent errand, but he has instructed me to take down in detail all you have to say.'

'You?' De Lacy's eyes widened with angry surprise.

Kishen nodded gently.

'Listen here, brown boy, I have no intention of dealing with the organ grinder's monkey. I am paying for the organ grinder in person.'

Kishen had prepared himself for this response. He had experienced a lifetime of similar abuse because of his colour, so the bruising outburst of an angry writer was not going to ruffle his feathers. In fact, he responded with a smile.

'Well, I may be a brown boy, Mr De Lacy, but that is no detriment to my intellectual capacity. And you must know that a monkey and organ grinder work as a team to achieve their aim, which is to entertain. Each is lost without the other. In our case, Mr Wilde and I work together in unison to solve mysteries. I can assure you that I am quite competent to deal with this matter on behalf of Mr Wilde who will be made aware in full detail of all that passes between us.'

Kishen's soothing tones and reasonable response surprised De Lacy. He wasn't expecting such an assured and confident reaction to his outburst, one which caused him to reconsider.

In this moment of hesitation, Kishen took his arm and led him to an armchair. 'You told Mr Wilde there had been developments. Something happened yesterday to alarm you further.'

'Yes. Last night,' De Lacy found himself saying, while roughly shaking off the young Indian's hand.

'Tell me all. As you do so I will make detailed notes,' Kishen said, remaining calm while grabbing a pad and pencil from the coffee table.

There was another hesitant pause, and De Lacy stared blankly at Kishen, who smiled and gave a gentle nod of encouragement.

De Lacy heaved a sigh and related the events that occurred at his apartment the previous night with the visit of Anthony Carfax.

'Has Carfax approached you for a loan before?'

'The odd fiver perhaps. 'Can you help me out? I seem to be short of change, old chap.' That sort of thing but never a demand for such a large sum.'

'He is a regular gambler?'

De Lacy gave a derisive snort. 'Inveterate. If you know what that means.'

'I do.'

'He always seems to be in some scrape regarding his betting activities, but I had no idea his gambling had got out of control like this.'

'Have you any idea to whom he is in debt for these two hundred pounds?'

'I do not. No doubt it is some low-life crooked bookie or dubious syndicate operating on the edge of the law.'

'You say he was fearful for his life.'

'That was the implication, but I am fairly sure he was over-egging the pudding. After all, he has paintings, ceramics, other items of value which could be sold. Why come to me? Those he owes money to are not likely to kill the golden goose, who will no doubt lay them more precious eggs in the future. I think a severe beating up, a busted nose, and a couple of black eyes is more likely.'

'Still not pleasant.'

'The penalties of playing with fire.'

'So, do you take his threat to you seriously?'

'I don't know. Under the circumstances, I am apprehensive. It may just be a wild frustrated outburst in response to my refusal to cough up the cash, but in this situation, bearing in mind the threatening letter, it gives one leave for thought. A threat is a threat, after all.'

Kishen nodded. 'Have you experienced any animosity from Lord Carfax before last night?'

'Not particularly. He's always been a cold fish with an artificial bonhomie that never fooled me, and I do suspect he is somewhat jealous of my success as a novelist.'

'On the surface, I would suggest....'

'*You* would suggest....'

'Indeed, I would. As the monkey partner I have my own views and perceptions, which are valid and pertinent to this investigation.' There was now a little steel in Kishen's voice, and his features had hardened.

De Lacy realised he had seriously underestimated the fellow. 'Well...,' he said somewhat awkwardly, "on the surface,' what do you suggest?'

Kishen's gentle demeanour returned. '...that we alert Lord Carfax that we are cognisant of his threat to you and warn him of the consequences of taking the matter further. That should prevent him from carrying out any rash act. I do not know the gentleman, but as you relate the incident, it seems that the threat came as simply a frustrated outburst because you refused to provide him with a loan. It does not appear that he has any other reason to harm you, and it is unlikely that he is connected with the poisonous letter that you received. Rest assured Mr Wilde, and I will consider this matter further, but it seems to me there is no real connection between Lord Carfax's warning and the letter you received.'

57

De Lacy could not argue with this assessment, not without revealing that he had received a second note just after Carfax had left his apartment—a note that held that dreaded phrase 'REMEMBERING DANIEL AND ROSEMULLION'. That must remain a secret, otherwise, Pandora's box would burst wide open.

While this interview was taking place, an interview which later Kishen, in his usual understated manner, described as being 'a touch awkward', Rupert Wilde was busy carrying out a spot of burglary. Safe in the knowledge that Ambrose De Lacy was ensconced with Kishen in his own apartment, Wilde was taking the opportunity to snoop around the author's abode. De Lacy lived in a large second-floor apartment at Grandchester House in Chelsea. Wilde was hoping to learn a little more about his intriguing client. He was fairly convinced that the famous writer was keeping something back, not revealing the whole picture regarding himself and his history. Wilde was sure that De Lacy's life was in danger, but for what reason was still not clear. He hoped that having a snoop around the man's quarters, peering into cupboards, rifling through drawers, seeking out hiding places, etc, may well reveal something which would help to illuminate the situation regarding this threat to his client's life.

Wilde's first task, once he had effected an entry, was to gauge the geography of the apartment. There was a narrow hallway leading into a sumptuous sitting room which included a spacious dining alcove. There was a neat kitchen, a large bedroom, a petite bathroom, and a book-lined study where obviously De Lacy did his writing. Wilde started with the sitting room, giving it a broad sweep. There didn't seem to be much here that would bring fresh information to the investigative table. There was a small bookcase filled mainly with De Lacy's own volumes along with some Dickens and Conan Doyle. A number of attractive oil paintings adorned the walls, all featuring rural settings. However, Wilde did spot a wastepaper basket placed under the table which housed the telephone. He examined the contents, and to his surprise, he extracted a screwed-up envelope and its contents. He smoothed out the sheet of notepaper and read the words 'REMEMBERING DANIEL

AND ROSEMULLION' etched neatly in capital letters. The writing, ink, notepaper, and envelope were identical to the threatening letter De Lacy had shown him. Why had this been thrown away? Obviously, he was not meant to see it. Why was that? What secret did this apparently innocent phrase mean to De Lacy that he was determined he should not discover it? Certainly, the words meant nothing to Wilde at the moment, but he was confident that he would, by hook or by crook, find out its relevance. And he was aware that he had to do this without De Lacy knowing. He was tempted to slip the sheet of paper into his pocket but thought better of it. He really did not want Mr Mystery Writer to know he had been sniffing about the place. However, Wilde was convinced that this discovery was important and made his burglarising trip worthwhile.

He next turned his attention to De Lacy's study. The desk was piled high with papers, some of which were pages from the novel he was working on currently. There were a few bills and notebooks filled with plot details. The wastepaper bin by the side of the desk was empty. In one of the drawers of the desk, he found a pencil sketch of a cottage. It was a fairly amateurish drawing but not completely without charm. Wilde made a mental note of the image and carried on with his search, but despite giving the room a very detailed survey, he failed to come up with anything that appeared unusual or in some way relevant to the case.

The bedroom was next. As he expected, the décor tended towards the exotic and feminine, with purple silk sheets adorning the bed. Again, this room provided nothing of note. Well, almost nothing. There was a small picture frame on the bedside table which contained a photograph. Wilde picked it up and studied it carefully. The photograph was of a very handsome young man with dark wavy hair and in possession of a devilish smile. There was a signature at the bottom: 'With love from D.' This was obviously one of De Lacy's lovers. Certainly, it was someone he really cared about enough for him to have pride of place at his bedside. Wilde would have liked to have taken the photograph away with him to aid his investigations, but he knew this was impossible. It was imperative that De Lacy had no notion that anyone had been in his flat. Nevertheless, he extracted the photograph from the frame and examined the back. He was delighted to see the name of the photographic studio and the bonus of a reference number added in pencil. He made a note of these before replacing the portrait in the frame. Then Wilde made a quick drawing of the man's face in his notepad. He wasn't an overly talented artist, but he could sketch a fair likeness. It was, he mused, better than nothing.

As he slipped the pad back in his coat pocket, he asked himself the inevitable question: who was this D, and did he feature in the case in any way? Could he be the Daniel referred to in the discarded note? And what did the word 'Rosemullion' mean?

Wilde completed his survey of the flat with a visit to the kitchen, which revealed nothing of importance. It was clean and well-organised but the pristine nature of the stove, lack of vegetables, and sparseness of tinned goods, seasoning and cooking paraphernalia seemed to indicate that De Lacy took most of his cooked meals out. Dining in restaurants—the privilege of a successful author.

He did a quick check to make sure that he was leaving the place exactly as he'd found it and was making his way to the door when he heard the key turn in the lock.

'Oh, Lord,' he gasped, dropping to his knees and peering around the corner as the door began to open very slowly. This was an unforeseen circumstance. Surely De Lacy hadn't failed to turn up for his appointment at his apartment and had returned...? What the hell!

As the door swung open slowly, a darkened silhouette appeared in the aperture. Wilde could make out the spindly shape of a short woman who was carrying a large shopping bag and muttering to herself.

Wilde felt a surge of relief. At least it wasn't the master of the house returning, but, most likely, the cleaner ready to spruce up the dwelling for Mr De Lacy. However, her presence provided Wilde with a problem: that of escaping without revealing his presence. He reasoned swiftly that the first thing the lady would do was visit the kitchen and make herself a nice cup of tea before tackling her domestic chores.

As she turned to close the door, chuntering to herself, Wilde moved like a phantom across the sitting room, around the corner into the bathroom. After waiting a few minutes, he emerged slowly and, crouching low, approached the sitting room once more. To his dismay, he saw the woman sprawled on the sofa, smoking a cigarette and cradling a glass of what he assumed was whisky or brandy. What the hell was he to do now? Well, logic told him that he had to wait for her to finish her smoke and then see what she would do next. Infuriatingly, she took an unconscionable amount of time savouring her cigarette. Stubbing the tab end out in a silver ashtray, she gave a little cough and rose inelegantly to her feet. To Wilde's horror, she began to move in his direction. In desperation, he retreated and slipped into the bedroom, praying that this was not the woman's destination. He hoped she was paying a visit to the bathroom. He waited anxiously, dreading the possibility of the door opening and being forced to make the rather comic and inelegant gesture of dropping to his knees and hiding under the bed.

There was silence for a time, and then he heard the lavatory flush. After a few moments, he opened the door a crack and peered out into the sitting room. To his amused surprise, he saw that the old lady had replenished her glass and was smoking another cigarette while reclining once again on the sofa.

He made a light-hearted note to himself not to employ this lazy soul as his cleaner. More importantly, he mused, how on earth am I going to exit this flat without being observed? The only way out was passing through the sitting room to the hall and then freedom. However, the smoking, alcohol-swilling gatekeeper was preventing such an escape.

Suddenly, the old lady gave a sigh and gently slumped sideways, her head resting on one of the embroidered cushions that adorned the sofa. Within seconds she was emitting a series of gentle snoring noises.

Thank the Lord, thought Wilde and, taking a deep breath, he slipped swiftly from the bedroom and headed for the front door. As he passed sleeping beauty, she emitted a loud grunt, and for a fleeting moment, her eyes flickered open only to close once again in slumber.

It was with immense relief that Rupert Wilde let himself out of the flat into the cool air of the corridor. That, he reckoned, with chagrin, was not one of my most efficient escapades.

Chapter Fourteen

Once out on the street, Wilde found a phone box and rang his flat. 'Hello, chum, how did the meeting with the celebrated author go?' he asked Kishen.

'A touch awkward, as you can imagine. He was quite annoyed you were not there to deal with his woes but once we settled down it was, I suppose, better than expected. I believe I rose to the occasion.'

Wilde smiled. 'I am sure you did. Perhaps I should start preparing for my retirement.'

'Oh, I think that would be a little premature.'

'Did you learn anything of interest to the case?'

'I'm not absolutely sure.' Kishen relayed the details of the interview he'd had with De Lacy and the author's concern about the threat made to him by Anthony Carfax. 'I wasn't sure whether there was any real cause for concern in the matter, but I thought it best to convince Mr De Lacy that it was no doubt an idle threat prompted by anger.'

'I expect that you are correct and you did the right thing in trying to allay the old bird's concerns. We can look into this business later.'

'What about your adventures?' asked Kishen

'Possibly fruit bearing. I'll tell you all when I get back, but I have another errand to perform first, so you'll be lunching on your own today. I will see you later this afternoon.'

The errand in question was a visit to Montgomery's Photographic Studio in Bayswater, the establishment which had produced the portrait that stood on Ambrose De Lacy's bedside table. With his fine broad handsome features and lustrous wavy hair, the subject of the portrait was obviously a gilded youth adored by the author.

Montgomery's had a discreet doorway in a charming side street just off Queensway, down from the main Bayswater Road. The walls of the reception area were adorned with numerous portraits of men, women, and families all staring out at Wilde with strange fixed unsmiling expressions. It seemed there was no joy in the process of posing; it was a serious gloomy business. A young woman was in attendance at the reception desk. She looked up at Wilde's approach and gave him a broad welcoming smile. The hairs prickled on the back of his neck. She was beautiful. A pure English rose, he thought. Large blue eyes which sparkled with intelligence, perfectly formed features with a smooth clear skin, and a slim, alluring, almost boyish figure. For a few moments, he was lost for words, entranced by this captivating creature. Attractive women had this effect on him.

'Hello,' she said softly. 'How may I help you?' Even her voice had seductive charm.

It was a good question, Wilde thought, so mesmerised by her that, for the moment, he had temporarily forgotten why he was there. When he did not respond, the young woman raised a delicate eyebrow in query.

'Yes, yes, hello,' he said awkwardly, pulling himself together. 'I'm trying to trace a missing person, a young man, someone who had his photograph taken here.'

She did not reply, just granting him a gentle quizzical look as she waited for further information.

'I have the reference number of the photograph....'

'Not the photograph?' she said.

He shook his head. 'Sadly, no.' Rather clumsily, Wilde extracted the sheet of paper from his pocket with the number. 'I wondered if you could check your records and let me have any details you may have regarding the sitter: name, address, and such like.'

The girl frowned. 'Name? You don't know the name?' She seemed surprised, suspicious even. Wilde admitted to himself that it did seem an odd request.

He shook his head gently in response to her question. 'The first name may well be Daniel, but I cannot be sure.'

'Are you a policeman?'

'In a manner of speaking. I am a private detective.' He smiled, hoping it would add some legitimacy to his request.

The young woman's eyes widened. Indeed, she seemed impressed. This encouraged Wilde to pass her one of his cards, which she read with interest.

'It must be quite an exciting job,' she said.

'Sometimes. There is a lot of routine business involved, though.'

'Like visiting photographic studios in search of mysterious missing men.'

Wilde gave a little chuckle. 'I suppose so. I'm trying to trace this man because I believe he can aid us with our enquiries. Are you able to help me?'

She pursed her lips and studied his card again. 'I'll see what I can do,' she said at length and, scooping up the paper, she disappeared into the room beyond.

She returned five minutes later, her face flushed with excitement. 'You are in luck, Rupert Wilde,' she said enthusiastically. 'I've managed to find the details that you require. I've jotted them down for you.' She handed him his sheet of paper. 'The photograph was taken five years ago, in 1916. The young man is Daniel Collins, and his address at that time was 32A St Alban's Avenue, Chiswick.

'Thank you. You are a marvel, Miss....'

'I'm Sally. Sally Peters.'

'Well, Sally Peters, you've been a great help.'

'It was quite exciting to be involved in a mystery, helping a private investigator. In a way, it was like being Watson to your Sherlock Holmes.' She grinned. 'I am a great fan of detective stories.'

Wilde was captivated by her beauty and her wonderfully animated features. 'Well, I'm no Sherlock, but I appreciate your assistance.'

'Is the man you're after some sort of villain, a ne'er do well?'

'That is something I have yet to establish. He is just a vague cog in the case I'm investigating at the moment.'

'Sounds fascinating.' The voice was low and enticing. It was topped by a sweet smile.

Wilde blushed. He was out of his depth. Females were an unknown quantity to him. Apart from a brief dalliance with a girl in his teens, he had not really had any serious relationship with a member of the opposite sex.

'Thank you so much for your help,' he said awkwardly, turning to leave, and then upon reaching the door, he suddenly changed his mind. He spoke again almost automatically as though his brain had not quite processed his thoughts or knew what he was saying. 'Pardon me, I hope I am not being sort of presumptuous, but I wondered...I wondered if you would care to take dinner with me some evening.' He couldn't believe he had said that, but he had.

She was in no way non-plussed by his offer. Indeed, she seemed pleased and, without any hesitation, gave a gentle nod of acceptance. 'That sounds lovely.'

'Tonight?'

She shook her head. 'I'm sorry, but I have other commitments this evening.'

'Tomorrow then?' He realised he was sounding desperate and pushy now.

'Yes. Tomorrow would be fine.'

'How about dinner at the Café Royal at seven-thirty. I will meet you in the foyer. Is that acceptable?'

Sally grinned. 'That is very acceptable.' She looked down and consulted his visiting card once more. 'Mr Rupert Wilde.'

As he left the photographic studio and felt the cool breeze on his face, Wilde didn't know quite how he felt. He was elated that he'd managed to arrange a date with a pretty young woman. Although he had only just met Sally, he felt as though he already knew her. There was humour and intelligence in her eyes that appealed to him, and her smile was entrancing. Nevertheless, he was surprised that he had summoned up his nerve to ask her out and wondered where the impetus had come from. It certainly wasn't like him to be so bold with the opposite sex. Well, he'd gone and done it now, and the full realisation of this brought a broad smile to his lips. Dinner at the Café Royal with Sally Peters. How wonderful.

By the time he reached his apartment, Wilde was ravenous and, while he set about making himself a large beef sandwich and grabbing a glass of cold beer, he told Kishen of his adventures and discoveries made at De Lacy's flat and the information he had obtained at the photographic studio. However, he deliberately failed to mention his attraction to the young lady who worked there and the date he had arranged with her the following evening. He felt too embarrassed to pass on the news of this romantic tryst—if indeed it was a romantic tryst. He felt rather like a schoolboy hiding a secret crush.

'So,' said Kishen, after Wilde had concluded his recital,' as I see it, we now have two avenues to explore: we take a visit to Chiswick, to the address you've been given, and see if we can find this Daniel Collins and we also need to interview Lord Carfax.'

'Nail firmly whacked on head, old boy,' said Wilde before attacking his beef sandwich.

Chapter Fifteen

It was growing dusk when Wilde drew his roadster to a halt on Chiswick High Road. 'We'll take it on foot from here, Kishen.'

'Whatever you say.'

'According to my A to Z of London, St Alban's Avenue is located somewhere in that direction.' Wilde flung his arm out, indicating the way. They set off with a will and soon located the address in question, which was situated on a broad tree-lined avenue. It was a semi-detached villa which had been converted into two separate flats. 32A was the ground floor property. Although the curtains were drawn, they could see that there were lights on inside. The resident was obviously at home.

This is too easy, thought Wilde, but kept the notion to himself as he rang the bell. If they were to encounter the mysterious Daniel, the case would open up beautifully like a rose in full bloom. Sadly, Fate rarely was this kind in a complicated investigation.

In due course, the door was opened by a short, rosy-cheeked man, aged, Wilde guessed, somewhere in his thirties. He was holding the evening paper in his hand. It was quite obvious this was not the man in the portrait, the mysterious 'D'.

'Yes?' he enquired, not unpleasantly.

'We're looking for Daniel Collins.'

The man gave a dark smirk. 'You're not the only ones. It's a bit late in the game now, I'm afraid.'

'Oh, why is that?'

'He's disappeared—become the invisible man. Evaporated into the ether.'

The man waved his newspaper about as though he was in the process of swatting a fly.

'I don't quite understand,' said Wilde with an assumed air of puzzlement. He wanted more specific details, and he reckoned this fellow could supply them if gently prompted.

'Owe you money does he… did he?'

Wilde decided to play along. 'Well, yes. How did you know?'

'Because over the last few years, I've had quite a few chaps like yourself trying to trace young master Collins. Bookies, loan sharks, tailors, wine merchants, etc., etc. He must have had a list of debts as long as your arm. He certainly seemed to like living the high life… on credit. Well, friend, I can tell you that you might as well say goodbye to your loot. There's not a cat in hell's chance of you getting it back.'

'If only I can find him.'

'Look, be told. You won't. One day he was living here, and the next, he had gone, disappeared without a trace. Even left some of his clothes here. Nobody knows where he went. The police and others have tried to locate him without any success whatsoever. There is a theory that he skipped to the continent. Maybe he was trying to avoid his call-up for the war. Apparently, he had been conscripted. Maybe he couldn't face having a go at the Hun, unlike some.' He tapped his chest with some force. 'It's likely he did a runner like so many of the bloody cowards. Well, I can tell you there has been no sign of him for five years. Whatever trail he left—and I believe he didn't leave as much as a fingerprint—that trail will be as cold as ice by now.'

'I see. Did you know him?'

The man shook his head. 'Not personally. I used to live nearby and saw him sometimes in the street. I've always fancied this particular apartment, and when it became vacant after Mr Houdini had done his vanishing act, I grabbed it.'

'So, he left nothing behind that would give any clue as to his whereabouts.'

'None that I know of. As I said, there were some nice suits but nothing else. Certainly, no cash. The police did a thorough search of the premises, and they got nowhere.'

'Well, thank you for putting us in the picture. It looks like we've got a lost cause on our hands.'

'Definitely. My advice is to forget about the matter. It can't be all that important after five years. Don't fritter your time trying to find Daniel Collins. It is a futile pursuit.'

'Well, that was a wasted journey,' said Kishen with a sigh as they made their way back towards the car.

'Not quite, old lad,' replied Wilde. 'Where there's a mystery, there must be some way of unravelling it. I reckon if I have a word with my chum Johnny Ferguson at Scotland Yard about the matter, we may learn a little more about the mysterious Mr Collins.'

'I suppose so, but wouldn't it be easier to simply raise the matter with Ambrose De Lacy?'

Wilde shook his head. 'Not at the moment. I think it is imperative that we do not reveal to him that we know of his connection with Collins. I'm sure that if we mentioned this Daniel fellow, he would clam up like the proverbial oyster or, worse, come up with some prefabricated fairy tale. Our client is harbouring secrets, secrets that he does not wish to reveal to us for some reason. If we were meant to know about this young, good-looking man, a picture of whom graces De Lacy's bedside cabinet, he would have told us about him already. No, my dear Kishen, it is our job to unearth these secrets ourselves so that we can put them in context with this case, the threatening letters, and so on.'

'So, what do we do about that?'

'A think a trip to Somerset House may throw a little more light on the Collins family.'

'And what about Lord Carfax?'

'Indeed, what about Lord Carfax? I reckon we should pay his Lordship a visit just to clear up the matter of his threatening behaviour. Tomorrow morning is perhaps best.' Wilde consulted his watch. 'No doubt at this time of the evening, he will be gallivanting about town, indulging himself in some club or other. I think it would be most advantageous if we catch his Lordship sober and a little bleary-eyed from sleep in order for us to extract the best responses from him.'

'I suspect he will be a late riser.'

'Right you are. A little before noon should be the most appropriate time to call. Now then, Kishen, we've had a busy and fairly productive day. How about a relaxing dinner somewhere we can put aside business concerns for an hour or two?'

'Both I and my rumbling tummy agree with your suggestion,' grinned Kishen.

Chapter Sixteen

Lord Carfax sat in a quiet bar in Soho nursing a scotch whisky. He felt wretched and full of self-pity. His life seemed to be crumbling about him. Because of his reckless extravagances, he was heading for penury. He had been forced to release most of the staff from his service. The cook, the maid, the footman had all gone. Only Rogers, his manservant, had survived the cull but, Carfax had to admit, even his tenure was fragile. He'd had to grant the old boy a month's leave in order to ease his expenses for a while. He was now living for a time in that grand mausoleum of a house on his own. His publishers had refused to give him an advance on his next, as yet unwritten, novel and that bastard De Lacy wouldn't dip into his spoils to lend him the beastly two hundred pounds he so desperately needed to pay off his gambling debt. In the end, he had been forced to sell a set of treasured silver goblets to acquire the funds to save his neck. The Italian to whom he owed the money had a set of rather unpleasant friends and he had been informed in graphic detail what they would do to him if he failed to come up with the cash.

Carfax took a long slug of whisky, allowing it to burn his throat. The discomfort gave him a kind of perverse pleasure. Well, he mused, by saying goodbye to my favourite goblets, I escaped an unpleasant beating. For the moment, I am still in one piece sans black eye, broken ribs, bruises, and with all my fingers intact. For this, I must be duly thankful. But where the hell do I go from here?

Another slug of whisky. The alcohol was beginning to work and he felt the burden of his crippled life ease somewhat, enough to allow him a slow sardonic smile. I suppose I'd better get that bloody book written so the blasted publishers will cough up the shekels, he told himself. His smile widened. A decision made. But there was a problem: he had no notion of a plot. 'That is a bit of a dilemma, Tony, old boy,' he murmured softly to himself with facetious glee before draining his glass.

On unsteady legs, he made his way home. He was totally unaware of the dark shadow following in his wake. Carfax stood before his house shrouded in darkness, conscious of the gloomy emptiness that awaited him inside. 'Hello, house,' he addressed the imposing silhouette softly. 'It was the silver goblets today, but it could be you in the near future if my fortunes don't improve.'

As he fumbled for his door key, he had no notion that his fortunes were very soon to take a turn for the worse. Much worse.

He let himself in and switched on a table lamp in the sitting room before heading for the drinks trolley. 'One little, no, one large nightcap, the balm of hurt minds, before I try to escape my woes in sleep,' he murmured.

He had just poured himself a large brandy when he thought he heard a noise behind him in the darkness beyond the sepulchral glow of the table lamp. He turned swiftly, stumbling a little as he did so. His eyes scanned the shadows looking for the source of the noise. He saw nothing but the sound came again.

'Who's there?' he called, his hand gripping his glass tightly with nervous apprehension.

'Friend or foe,' came a whisper from the darkness.

'Who the hell are you?' cried Carfax, starting to panic now.

'Foe,' came the reply.

Out of the blackness, a figure emerged slowly, illuminated gently by the outer rays of the lamp. It was a cowled figure who wore a mask. It was the mask of a skull.

'Who the hell are you? What are you doing here?' asked Carfax, his voice a nervous hoarse croak. He stumbled forward towards the figure. ''What do you want?'

'You,' came the reply. Then without warning the intruder rushed forward and lunged at Carfax, raising its right arm, which held some bulky object. Carfax was mesmerised by this vision. Fear and alcohol held him frozen to the spot. With an inarticulate cry, the figure brought the weapon down with some force on Carfax's forehead. There was an awful cracking sound and the writer opened his mouth to scream, but no sound emerged. He fell silently to the ground, the brandy glass flying through the air.

The intruder knelt over the inert body and brought his weapon down on his victim's head several times, more than was necessary to be assured that the man was dead.

Mission accomplished the intruder made their way to the front door, chuckling as they did so.

'As a student of literary crime, Kishen, old chap, have you ever dipped into any of Anthony Carfax's efforts?' Rupert Wilde made this casual query as he and his associate journeyed to Carfax's house in Wilde's roadster the following morning.

'I'm afraid not, but after our encounter today, perhaps I should.'

'As research, eh? Well, no doubt you can gather some clues as to the character and attitudes from an author's writings but we are more likely to gather more insight in a face-to-face interview this morning.'

Carfax's townhouse was situated in Chelsea, one of a row of large, impressive buildings whose façades spoke of wealth and privilege. On reaching the front door, they were surprised to find it slightly ajar. After a quick exchange of surprised glances, Wilde rang the bell. The jangling tintinnabulation echoed eerily through the house. They waited in vain for a response.

After a few minutes, Wilde pushed open the door and stepped inside. 'Hello,' he called out. His cry was greeted with silence.

'This is a funny business. Surely there should be a maid or manservant somewhere responsible for answering the door,' he observed.

'It is strange indeed,' Kishen agreed.

Stepping further into the hall, Wilde called out again, the words echoing in the stillness. Once more, there was no response. He turned to Kishen.

'There is something wrong here,' he said.

Without further words, both men moved slowly down the hall. There was a dull yellow glow emanating from a room to their right. It was here that they discovered the body of Lord Carfax. He lay on his back, his head circled by a halo of congealed blood. His shattered skull was exposed, resembling a crimson sponge. It was clear to Wilde that he had been attacked violently from the front with a heavy object. Lying, some three feet away was the culprit: a heavy onyx ashtray, which was also covered in blood.

'Oh, my goodness,' Kishen exclaimed, his hand flying up to his mouth. 'Murder.'

'Indeed, murder most foul,' observed Wilde as he knelt down by the corpse. 'Bludgeoned to death. There's not much of the skull left. The poor devil didn't stand a chance. Rigor mortis has only just begun to set in, so it is most likely that he was killed in the early hours of this morning.'

'Such violence,' said Kishen staring with unease at the vicious wounds.

'Yes, there is ferocity and anger here. I'm afraid our case has just turned a very dark corner.'

'Surely Ambrose De Lacy is not responsible?'

Wilde heaved a deep sigh. 'I don't know... yet. On the surface, it seems improbable, but it is not without precedent that the most obvious suspect is also the guilty one.' Wilde rose to his feet. 'Whatever the case, this has become a police matter now. Did you notice a telephone anywhere?'

Detective Inspector Johnny Ferguson was just enjoying a mid-morning cup of tea and a couple of digestive biscuits while he studied some case notes on his desk when his phone rang. His face briefly registered a flicker of irritation at being disturbed at this quiet time of the morning. With a sigh, he lifted the receiver and gave his name.

'Hello, Johnny. Rupert Wilde here,' came the response.

Ferguson's features lightened, and he smiled. 'Rupert, you son of a gun, how are you? Not seen your ugly mug for months. What can I do for you?'

'It's more what I can you for you, Johnny. I have a body you may be interested in.'

Within an hour, Ferguson and his sergeant, Bob Sanders, were standing over the dead body of Anthony Carfax.

'Very nasty,' the policeman observed. 'You say this fellow is a writer of detective stories.'

'He *was*, yes.'

'Any notions why he was killed and who might have done it?'

Wilde shook his head.

'I think you'd better tell me about your involvement in this affair and how you managed to be here at the scene of the crime.'

Wilde gave an edited resumé of the case so far. He did not mention the fact that De Lacy had received a threatening letter and intimated that the author had consulted him regarding Lord Carfax's dark warning after refusing to help pay his gambling debt.

Ferguson allowed the information to register for some moments. 'It seems as though your client, this De Lacy fellow, emerges as the key suspect for the moment.'

Wilde made no attempt to deny this assumption, but he was aware that there was more to uncover in this strange business before fingers of accusation could be pointed with accuracy.

Ferguson turned to his sergeant. 'Get the forensic team in here and then have the body removed, Bob. Meanwhile, I think I need to have a chat with Mr De Lacy.'

'Do you mind if Kishen and I tag along? He is our client, after all.'

Ferguson gave his friend a sardonic grin. 'I suppose not.'

Ambrose De Lacy was most surprised to find Rupert Wilde and his Indian associate, along with a tall, swarthy authoritative individual calling on him just as he was about to take a light lunch.

'Have there been developments in the case?' he asked in a brittle fashion, adding, 'and who is this gentleman?'

Wilde nodded. 'Yes, there have been serious developments, and this gentleman is Detective Inspector Ferguson of Scotland Yard.'

At this revelation, De Lacy's face paled. 'Scotland Yard,' he repeated. 'I don't understand.'

'I'm sorry to tell you that Anthony Carfax is dead,' said Wilde.

De Lacy's mouth opened in shock, and he slumped down into a chair. 'Dead? Good gracious. How?'

'He was murdered. Bludgeoned to death.' It was Ferguson who relayed this information. It was designed to be a brutal statement; the policeman wished to see how De Lacy would react.

The author groaned, shaking his head in disbelief. 'Great heavens,' he cried. He pulled himself from the chair. 'I need a drink.' Without another word, he poured himself a generous whisky and took a large gulp. 'Bludgeoned to death, you say. Who would do a thing like that?'

'Perhaps you may have some idea?' suggested Ferguson.

'Me. Why on earth should I? I write about murders. I know nothing about them in real life. Where was Carfax found?'

'In the sitting room of his own house.'

'Ah, an intruder. A burglar caught in the act lashes out. Surely that is the most obvious scenario.'

'Obvious but too simple,' observed Wilde. 'There appears to have been nothing taken and there was no sign of a forced entry. I am convinced that the intruder's sole purpose was murder.'

'Mr Wilde tells me that Lord Carfax had threatened you with violence the other evening because you refused to lend him a sum of money.'

De Lacy threw an accusative look at Wilde, clearly annoyed with him for revealing such personal details. 'Did he?' he snapped. 'That was a private matter.'

'Not quite, Mr De Lacy, not after what has happened.'

'What do you mean?'

Ferguson gave the author an indulgent smile. 'Don't be naïve, Mr De Lacy. We need to know more about the animosity between you and Carfax.'

'Animosity! You're not suggesting that I killed him.'

Ferguson did not rise to the bait of that question. 'I am simply assembling all the information that I can to help me solve this murder. When was the last time you saw Lord Carfax?'

'When he came here two nights ago trying to wheedle two hundred pounds from me to settle a gambling debt. I gave him short shrift. As you no doubt are aware, he threatened me, said I would regret my decision. I told Mr Wilde all about it, which was not a very sensible thing to do if I intended to kill the man. Indeed, Inspector, the idea is ridiculous.'

Again, Ferguson did not respond to this heated statement but continued with his questioning. 'Where were you last night?'

De Lacy pursed his lips with annoyance. 'If you must know, I dined at La Locanda, a favourite restaurant of mine....'

'Alone?'

'I invariably dine alone, but the staff know me there, and no doubt can vouch for my presence... if necessary.'

'And after the meal?'

'I walked home. I carried out some revision on the pages I'd written earlier in the day and then went to bed. Alone. You'll just have to take my word for it.'

'Of course. For the time being, at least. One final thing: you are certain you have no notion of anyone who would want Lord Carfax dead.'

De Lacy shook his head. 'No. Unless, of course, the people to whom he owed money took their revenge. I believe he was fearful of repercussions if he failed to come up with the cash to pay what he owed them. I did not think it would go to the extreme of murder.'

'Well, that is certainly something we will be looking into. That's all for the moment, but no doubt I will see you again.'

'I can hardly wait,' De Lacy sneered sarcastically.

Ferguson moved to go, taking Wilde's arm as he did so, leading him into the hallway for a quiet conversation.

'You've got an odd one there, Rupert.'

'Well, we're all odd to some people.'

Ferguson grinned. 'Oh, it's Rupert Wilde, the philosopher.'

'Or realist,' came Wilde's response, no smile but a twinkle in the eye.

'What do you reckon? Is he our man?'

Wilde shook his head. 'I don't think he did it. He's not the type, and besides, there is no real motive. What does he gain from Carfax's demise?'

'Well, nothing that is obvious, I agree. Look, I'll leave him alone for a while. He's your client, but keep me informed if anything surfaces. You know what I mean.'

Wilde tapped his old friend on the shoulder. 'Of course, I know what you mean. Rest assured, it shall be done. Trust me.'

Ferguson returned the tap on the shoulder. 'I do.'

'Actually, Johnny, there is something you can help me with. I am trying to trace a missing person and find out about his background. He disappeared about five years ago, and I suspect the police would have been involved initially in looking for him. A missing person case. He lived in Chiswick, and his name was Daniel Collins. Could you dig something up about him for me?'

Ferguson jotted down the name in his notebook. 'I'll see what I can do. Is this a missing link in your De Lacy investigation?'

Wide smiled. There was little that got past his old perceptive chum. He just gave a brief nod in reply.

'Leave it with me,' Ferguson said, pocketing his notebook. 'Business aside, we must have a drink together some evening. It's been too long.'

'Indeed. Soon.'

The two men parted with a shake of the hand.

Wilde returned to the sitting room where De Lacy sat morosely nursing a now empty glass. Kishen stood by uneasily, a look of relief brightening his features at his associate's return.

'This is a great mess, isn't it?' said De Lacy gloomily. 'Are we to assume that Carfax's murder has something to do with my threatening letter, or is it a completely different matter?'

'To be honest, I'm not sure,' said Wilde. 'When you last saw Carfax, did he intimate that he'd had a similar threat?'

De Lacy shook his head.

'And you've not had another such missive?'

The author hesitated for a moment. It was an awkward gesture, and Wilde saw that he was about to lie, to deny the existence of the note he'd found in the wastepaper basket.

'You have, haven't you? I can see it in your eyes,' he snapped, irritated that De Lacy was still attempting to keep him in the dark. He was determined to force the author out into the open.

De Lacy's lips moved, but no sound came.

'When? When did you receive it?' Wilde pressed.

'Yesterday.' The admittance was muted.

'What did it say?'

Another hesitation. 'Just the same as the first.'

'Exactly the same message?'

'Yes.'

'Where is it? I'd like to see it.'

'I threw it away. It… It made me so angry.'

Kishen gave a little gasp. 'You threw it away. But it was evidence.'

De Lacy shrugged his shoulders. 'I told you: it was just the same as the first one. Identical. I couldn't bear to have it in the flat. If you must know, I burned it.'

There was silence for a moment before Wilde sighed heavily. 'So, with Lord Carfax out of the frame, I must ask you again, can you think who may be sending these messages?'

'No. No. No. I've told you. I have no idea.'

Wilde did not believe him, but if that was the way De Lacy wanted to play the game, he would let him—for the moment. In time he would have to come clean.

'Very well. There is little I can do to help you right now. We must wait for further developments.'

'You mean until someone murders me!' De Lacy was angry now, his face flushed with emotion.

Wilde knew in circumstances like this, it was a mistake to rise to match De Lacy's anger. A calm, sensible response uttered in a reasonable voice often deflated the balloon of rage.

'You must be vigilant at all times. You must inform me of anything that happens to you that is out of the ordinary, and certainly, you must not destroy any further letters you receive. If you behave in this sensible fashion, I am sure we can get to the bottom of this strange affair without any harm coming to you. But it is essential that you co-operate with me. You must trust me. Is that understood?' He was tempted to add, 'And would you kindly tell me what 'Remember Daniel' means to you? And how does Daniel Collins fit into this melodrama?' But he held back. Now was not the time to deal with this. It was best to keep this nugget of information to himself for the time being.

After a brief pause, De Lacy's body slumped as he digested Wilde's wise words. Indeed, the balloon of anger had been successfully deflated. 'Very well,' he said, almost graciously.

'Good. We will contact you each morning to check that there haven't been any developments overnight. However, if anything does happen, contact me or Kishen immediately.'

'Don't forget you are a guest at the Murder Club the day after tomorrow. No doubt it will be a strange meeting. The death of Carfax will have shocked the members, and we shall have speeches and a toast to our departed colleague. As soon as the news is out in the evening papers, I expect my telephone will be red hot.'

On leaving De Lacy's apartment, Kishen could barely contain his curiosity. 'Why on earth did you not quiz our client about that fellow in the photograph, Daniel Collins? Surely, with the death of Lord Carfax it is even more important to unearth all De Lacy's secrets?'

'I agree,' said Wilde, 'but we have to do that for ourselves. We'll never get a straight answer from our friend Ambrose. If he had been prepared to tell us all about Daniel Collins, he would have done so by now. I've asked Johnny to sniff around the matter of young Daniel's disappearance and see what he can dig up. That may give us a lead.'

'And in the meantime…?'

'We wait for developments. Oh, and that reminds me, I'm dining out with…with an old friend this evening, so why don't you treat yourself to a trip to one of your concerts or the flicks.'

'Well, yes,' said Kishen, somewhat surprised by this sudden announcement. 'An old friend, you say. Who is that?'

'Oh, someone you don't know. A fellow from my army days.' Wilde was surprised at how easily the lie slipped out while, at the same time, he experienced a twinge of guilt deceiving Kishen in this way. The strange thing was that he really didn't know why he had spouted an untruth. He could so easily have said, 'I am meeting a pretty young woman for dinner,' but for some deep-seated reason, he shied away from it.

Chapter Seventeen

The mind of a murderer is a curious thing. It allows them to view the world in a dark and simplistic fashion where death—someone else's death - brings satisfaction, pleasure and a strange kind of closure, especially if there is deep hatred and a burning desire to wreak revenge. These elements are strong and more incalculable if the brain is clinically unstable. Then the whole of the life of the murderer is dictated by the twisted concepts created by this damaged brain. The world is viewed as though through a cracked distorting mirror.

So it was with the individual who had killed Lord Carfax and sent the warning notes to Ambrose De Lacy. Ah, Ambrose De Lacy. He was the real prize in this bloody game. He was the one to be saved until last. The grand finale, as it were. But Carfax had to be dealt with because he had muddied the waters and provided a threat to the murderer's plans. His Lordship's exclamation, 'I could kill you for this!' had been overheard. What if Carfax had meant it—that it wasn't simply prompted by alcohol or a sudden angry response, but a real threat.

Now there was a growing realisation that there were to be others to be dealt with also. More than had been originally imagined. But that was not seen as a problem for this twisted mind. Indeed, it was experiencing great pleasure in the 'killing spree' as they thought of it. It was pleasing to think that the more that were eliminated, the more De Lacy would squirm and shiver with fear. As he should. As he damned well should. Death was one thing, the anticipation of it as it crept nearer brought greater distress and pain. And more pleasure to me, thought the murderer.

So, who was to be next? Who indeed? Well, it wasn't a difficult question. The answer was logical. Another pale shadow had appeared on the horizon bringing with it a threat to the carefully prepared plans. It was a shadow that was likely to grow darker and more significant unless it was dealt with. He was the fly in the smooth ointment. It was imperative that this fellow did not hinder the final *coup de grace*—the elimination of that trumped-up old hack. In the end, that is what it was all about. And this person on the scene was likely to get in the way.

And so, that private detective had to be dealt with. And swiftly.

Chapter Eighteen

As Rupert Wilde approached the Café Royal that evening, he felt as nervous and tense as he had done in the muddy trenches in France, anticipating another barrage from the Bosch. Taking a beautiful girl to dinner was such an alien activity to him. Despite his age, he had never done it formally before. There had been a few women in his life, but they were just casual affairs, youthful dalliances. There had been Elise, the French girl in the village where he had been stationed for a few weeks. That had been a passionate affair, but it was hardly a meeting of minds, rather a collision of bodies.

Wilde was a suave confident fellow in general, presenting an image of a sophisticated man about town. But he had an Achilles heel: he was totally at sea in the romance department. Part of him now wished he had not asked Sally to dinner, while another part was thrilled at the prospect. He just hoped that he wouldn't make an ass of himself.

Taking a deep breath, he passed through the gilded portals of the Café Royal into the warm womb of the foyer. He gazed around. She was not there. He consulted his watch. As was his practice, he had arrived on the dot. Well, he told himself, it was the lady's prerogative to be a little late. As he was trying to convince himself of this, he was approached by a sallow-faced individual in a stiff penguin suit.

'You are dining with us this evening, sir?'

'Yes.'

'You have made a reservation?'

'I have. Name of Wilde. A table for two. I am waiting for my guest.'

'Ah.' The sallow features formed a professional smile, and he slunk back to his post at the reception desk.

Wilde seated himself on a low banquette and lit a cigarette. Surely Sally would be here by the time he'd smoked it. Three cigarettes later and there was still no sign of her. Wilde allowed himself a wry grin. It looks like the lady is standing me up. Well, she had agreed to his offer of dinner without hesitation. That was probably because she had no intention of turning up. Or, at least, she'd had second thoughts about the arrangement. He glanced at his watch. It was just after eight. With a sigh, he rose and approached the reception desk. 'It looks like my friend can't make it, so I'll be dining alone.'

'I understand, sir.' There was a subtle smirk in the voice. 'Shall I take you through to your table?'

Once seated, Wilde was given a huge folder containing the menu. 'While I peruse this, I'd like a large gin with a gentle splash of tonic,' he told the waiter. He needed an intake of alcohol to help him make a decision. This was not in connection with his possible menu choices but with how he really felt about the non-appearance of Sally Peters. He was disappointed, of course, but he wondered if he was also experiencing a modicum of relief. He wasn't a coward by any means, but he had been terribly apprehensive concerning how he would cope with this assignation. For him, this was unknown territory. It was an expedition for which he felt very ill-equipped.

As he was taking a large gulp of the ice-cold gin, a voice close to his ear said, 'I see you've started without me.'

He glanced up at the speaker and saw the beautiful face of Sally Peters. She appeared before him like a mirage, dressed in a simple but fetching dark blue dress which set off her slim boyish figure wonderfully.

He was lost for words for a moment and then found himself saying, 'Hello,' as he rose to his feet to greet her.

'I'm so sorry I'm late, Rupert. My taxi broke down, and it took me ages to find another one. I expect you thought I wasn't coming.'

'Well….' He began, then hesitated, unsure how to respond. He didn't want to admit that he had given up on her. It seemed to him a kind of weakness if he did so. He was rescued by the arrival of a waiter who pulled out a chair for Sally. 'Welcome, miss,' he said. 'May I bring you a drink?'

'I think the lady may like a glass of champagne?' said Wilde, shrugging off all uncertainties, and raising an eyebrow as he looked at his dinner guest.

'That would be wonderful,' she said, beaming.

And so, the evening really began. After the somewhat awkward start, things went swimmingly. The food was excellent, and Wilde and Sally very quickly felt at ease in each other's company. He learned that she was the daughter of the owner/photographer of the Montgomery Studio, who had kept on the name of the original owner for the sake of continuity. She helped her father with his photographic work and managed the accounts. Rather than talk about herself—'just an ordinary girl, really' - she was more interested in Wilde's profession, but he was reluctant to go into details about his detective activities. Instead, he revealed something of his biography, making light of his time in the army, and told her of his relationship with Kishen. By the end of the meal, he was so relaxed that his own natural wit and charm were in full flow. To his delight, he was able to make his beautiful companion laugh.

'Did you manage to find your mysterious missing man—that Daniel whatsisname?' she asked at one point.

'Not yet, but I have hopes.'

'If you like, I can get my father to print another picture. We still have the negative.'

'That would be great. It could come in handy later.'

'I'll arrange it.'

'Thank you. Now, what do you fancy for dessert?'

It was after ten when Rupert Wilde and Sally Peters left the Café Royal. The cool night air was pleasant after the somewhat oppressive warmth of the restaurant. They were so wrapped up in the pleasure of each other's company that they did not see the silhouette of a tall figure loitering in the shadows a few yards away from the entrance. It moved a little closer to the couple to catch their conversation.

'Well, Mr Wilde,' said Sally smiling and clinging to his arm, 'that was a lovely evening.'

'Certainly was,' he replied, thrilling to the closeness of this beautiful creature. Her sweetness and enticing femininity were quite intoxicating. Certainly, to him, she was no 'ordinary girl.'

'I'll get a taxi and see you home.'

'Thank you.' She sighed. 'I suppose all good things must come to an end.'

At that time of night, Regent Street was alive with taxi cabs, and Wilde had no difficulty in flagging one down, and neither did the individual who had been waiting and watching in a nearby doorway.

Wilde and Sally said little on the taxi ride. This was not out of embarrassment or awkwardness but simply in the quiet pleasure of being close in each other's company without the need for conversation. Sally lived in Islington with her father, and soon, the taxi pulled up outside a pleasant-looking semi-detached villa.

'Well, here we are.' she said, somewhat unnecessarily.

'Yes,' agreed Wilde vaguely, wondering what he was to do now. Before he could make any decisions, Sally leaned forward and kissed him gently on the lips. 'Thank you for a lovely evening. I'd love to do it again sometime.'

Rather numbed by her sudden show of affection, Wilde could only nod at first, but as Sally moved to leave the cab, he pulled her back gently, and now he kissed her. 'I'll call you at the studio,' he said.

She squeezed his hand and disappeared into the night.

As the taxi drove off to take Wilde home, he sat back, a beatific smile on his face. He had never quite felt like this before. He was happy, he was puzzled, and he was strangely content. She liked him, and he liked her. How lovely was that?

Meanwhile, the stranger had taken down details of the young woman's address, the young woman whom they had overheard was called Sally. The young woman who was a close friend of that detective nuisance, Rupert Wilde.

Unaware of the dark shadow that was looming on his personal horizon, Wilde was still smiling when he let himself into his flat. Kishen was in the sitting room, reading a book. 'Ah, the wanderer returns. How was dinner with your old friend?' he asked casually, slipping a bookmark into the volume.

'Wonderful,' said Rupert, before he had time to check himself.

'Wonderful? Wow, what happened?'

'Oh, we just had a good time, catching up on things…y'know.'

'And that was 'wonderful?' Kishen looked a little puzzled at his friend's enthusiasm. Well, I'm glad you had a good time.'

'Oh, I did.'

Wilde slept uneasily that night. Too many thoughts were swirling round his brain. His emotion stirred excitedly by his feelings for Sally; his guilt at deceiving Kishen about his date; and his concerns for the De Lacy mystery, which didn't seem to be progressing as well as he'd hoped.

Chapter Nineteen

When all this started, the plan, the desire was to frighten Ambrose De Lacy into a state of gibbering fear before getting rid of the bastard, but as the machinations got underway, the stranger saw that they could extend the author's mental torture by eliminating others connected with him such as Carfax and the woman who indirectly had a hand in the matter that prompted this trail of revenge. However, the stranger now realised that the priority was to get rid of that interfering sleuth before he discovered things he shouldn't and edged himself towards the truth, ruining everything. It was a challenge, but it was a satisfying one. It was an extra pleasure in this fascinating game of murder. The stranger smiled at the thought of it.

Chapter Twenty

On waking, Wilde had decided that he was not going to prevaricate with Kishen any more concerning Sally. He was baffled as to why he had lied about his date with her in the first place. He wondered if he was too embarrassed to reveal that he could have a sentimental romantic side to his nature. After all, it was normal for a single fellow in his late twenties to have a lady friend. Whatever transpired between him and Sally would not interfere with his partnership with Kishen. Although they had become good friends, they were also a professional duo with a job to do.

Over breakfast, Wilde told Kishen the truth. He had not met an old military friend for dinner the previous evening but had taken a pretty young lady out for a meal at the Café Royal. Kishen chuckled at this revelation, a reaction which disconcerted Wilde.

'I am so happy to hear this,' said Kishen, a broad smile wreathing his features. 'You are starting to live again and maybe love again. I remember when you first appointed me as your assistant, you were still suffering from the mental scars of the war. You seemed to me to feel a little adrift in society, finding normal life rather awkward. You were on the bank, uncertain about whether or not to enter the water or even how to do it. Friendship with a young lady will bring you great ease.'

Wilde laughed. 'You have the mind of a sensitive poet, Kishen, old boy. However, don't go creating a romantic melodrama out of one evening meal. Nevertheless, I accept your observations because I know you to be an honest and perceptive soul. You are right, of course. It has taken me some time to slough off the mental shackles created by the war, but I'm getting there.'

'Indeed, you are, and I wish you well with Sally. You will be seeing her again?'

Wilde nodded. 'In due course, but in the meantime, we have this De Lacy business to clear up. Tonight will be interesting.'

'Ah, the Murder Club meeting. Are you prepared for that?'

'I'll make a few notes this morning, but I reckon I'm going to be flying by the seat of my pants. However, I'm sure I can come up with something extempore.'

'Well, your pants are very well tailored, so I'm sure that you will be fine. Are you certain you want me to accompany you? I expect that the only experience these distinguished authors have of an Indian boy in their presence is as a servant proffering them drinks on the veranda. Won't they be ruffled to have one sitting at their dining table?'

Wilde gave a thin smile. 'I hope so. Of course, I want you there. You will be my second pair of eyes. We must scrutinise the whole bunch to see if we extract some sort of clue, anything that will help us. With the murder of Carfax, it is beginning to look like the culprit could be one of these literary blighters, after all. Well, that's what the facts suggest, although I must admit my instincts still tell me otherwise.'

'Oh?'

'Don't ask me to explain or rationalise. I can't. Just a gut feeling—and they are not always reliable.'

'They usually are with you.'

'We'll see,' Wilde said lightly with a smile, far from convinced in his own mind that the tangled skein of this case was making much sense to him at the moment.

That evening Rupert Wilde and Kishen Chabra donned their evening suits in preparation for the Murder Club Dinner. As Kishen emerged from his room, his expression clearly indicated that he was not in the least looking forward to the event.

'I can't tempt you to a snifter to brighten your spirits before we depart?' said Wilde, pouring himself a stiff whisky.

Kishen shook his head. 'You know I am not permitted alcohol.'

'No exceptions?'

'No exceptions.'

The Garrick Club, founded in 1831, is a private members club situated in the heart of London's West End, named after the eminent 18th-century actor, playwright, and theatre manager. It has an important theatrical library, and the walls of the establishment are adorned with a collection of valuable theatrical drawings and paintings. Sir Henry Irving and Charles Dickens were amongst its notable past members. The current exclusive membership consisted of the rich and the artistic. Ambrose De Lacy was both, and so was a very welcome addition to the club's distinguished clientele.

After announcing themselves, a liveried footman showed them upstairs to the private dining room where the Murder Club members met and feasted. Kishen gazed at the paintings on the wall with great interest, most of which were portraits of actors in various roles in Shakespearian plays. He really would have liked to have been able to linger and study them in detail, but the servant was moving at a swift pace.

De Lacy greeted them as they entered, casting a somewhat jaundiced eye over Kishen. At least the fellow looks respectable enough in an evening suit, he mused to himself, 'Let me introduce you to the members—the remaining members of the Murder Club,' he said with somewhat forced bonhomie. 'We'll tackle the two gents by the bar first.' Taking Wilde by the arm, he led him forward, Kishen following in their wake.

'This is Jacob Brown, our rural crime writer,' De Lacy announced, indicating a fat, tweed-suited fellow with grizzled grey hair who was nursing a large glass of beer. 'And this young fellow is Professor Alan Watkins—he writes under the pseudonym of Adam Worth.'

Wilde thought that Watkins did indeed look like an academic with his round glasses perched on the end of his nose and his slightly unkempt hair, which fell carelessly across his forehead. There was also a kind of faraway look in those pale blue eyes, which seemed to suggest that his mind was elsewhere, strolling down the avenues of academe perhaps. He peered at

Wilde in a strange absent-minded fashion.

'And this, gentleman, is our guest speaker, Rupert Wilde,' announced De Lacy with a gentle gesture of the hand. The two writers gave nods and muted greetings. Wilde stood back and indicated Kishen. 'And my associate Kishen Chabra,' he said.

More nods.

'We've just been talking about Carfax, poor devil,' said Watkins, the voice dry as a faded manuscript, belying his youth. His cadences and accent indicated his Welsh origins.

Brown gave what Wilde took to be a gentle guffaw, unless he was clearing his throat. 'Indeed, commenting on the bloody irony of the whole thing. Here's a fellow who spends his time writing about murder, violent deaths, and such, and then the poor bastard ends up actually being bumped off himself in mysterious circumstances. A bloody fact that is stranger than our fictions, eh?'

'What do you make of it, Mr Wilde?' asked Watkins. 'I gather you were in at the kill, so to speak.'

Wilde shrugged. 'I know no more than you, I'm afraid. It is true that Kishen and I discovered the body, but that's all. The police took over the matter straight away, and we were out of the picture.'

Brown cast a steely gaze in Wilde's direction. 'What were you doing visiting Carfax in the first place?'

'Oh, you'll appreciate that I can't say. Confidentiality is essential in my line of work. But perhaps you have some inkling yourself as to why the man was murdered?'

'No idea whatsoever,' responded Brown brusquely, his broad shoulders rising and falling in a huge shrug.

Watkins smiled. 'Me neither. I have no knowledge of his private life.'

'But surely, you, Wilde have come to some conclusions about the matter,' said Brown, worrying at the subject like a dog with a bone.

Wilde gave a slight shake of the head.

De Lacy intervened before Brown could press the matter further. 'We must allow our private detective some discretion, Jacob.'

Brown raised a cynical eyebrow. 'Aye, I suppose—so then, Mr Wilde, you're not quite 'out of the picture' yet.'

Wilde responded with an enigmatic smile and then allowed De Lacy to guide him away towards the dining room table where the two other members of the Murder Club were sitting. These were Meg Granger, a young dark-haired woman who was, Wilde thought, wearing rather too much makeup. There was something about her restless eyes that was a little unsettling.

Sitting beside her was a stout woman in her fifties with short-cropped hair and a daunting pair of dark-rimmed spectacles, which made her look like an angry owl. De Lacy carried out the introductions again, and limp handshakes were made.

'I expect being a real-life detective is much more exciting than sitting at a typewriter thinking up mysteries,' observed Meg Granger.

'Well, detective work is not all shootouts in dark alleys or chasing crooks over rooftops. There are lots of boring and mundane moments also.'

Granger's bright red lips parted in a smile. 'Oh, how disappointing.' It was a comment tinged with sarcasm.

'For me, I get very excited tapping away at my old typewriter, creating scandalous crimes and convoluted mysteries,' observed Vivien Dowson with some gravity.

'Each to his own, I suppose,' said Kishen quietly.

The two women stared at him in gentle surprise as though they weren't expecting this Indian fellow to speak and even less voice an opinion.

'Good point,' said Vivien Dowson briskly after a pause. 'That's the way the world turns. Indeed, each to his own, everyone following their own talents and desires. I could no way solve a real-life murder mystery than I expect you, Mr Wilde, could write one.'

'That is true,' agreed Wilde with a smile.

'But no doubt you will observe characters, individuals, as we authors do, and form impressions of them and judge them,' said Meg Granger somewhat pointedly.

Wilde responded with a gentle smile. He wasn't about to be led down that thorny path.

'I wonder,' continued the young woman, 'what you make of us all. What you think of me, for instance?'

There was a brief awkward silence before Wilde replied. 'Do you know, I haven't quite made up my mind,' he said, retaining his gentle smile.

At this juncture, another woman joined the group. De Lacy took her hand. 'Ah, here she is, traditionally late as usual. Let me introduce you to Briony Lodge. Briony, this is our guest speaker Rupert Wilde...and his assistant Kishen Chabra.'

The woman gave them a nod of the head. 'Nice to meet you... both,' she said without much conviction. She was a tall, angular woman somewhere in her thirties, having a pleasant face with high cheekbones and large blue eyes. She wore a tight-fitting cocktail dress of cream silk patterned with little blue flowers, which emphasised her lean body. In her brief statement, Wilde had detected the Australian accent in her voice.

'Have you been in this country long?' enquired Wilde.

'Five years, I suppose. It's the miserable fog and rain I love so much.' She grinned at her own irony. 'But the British readers seem to like my stuff, so I stay.' She turned to Kishen. 'And what about you, fellow exile? How long have you been in this country?'

'I have been here for over twenty years. To me, England is home.'

'Good old Blighty, the international melting pot, eh?'

At this juncture, the head waiter arrived to inform De Lacy that dinner was about to be served. As the group began moving to the dining table, Meg Granger took Wilde's arm gently and pulled him to one side. 'How well do you know Ambrose?' she said almost in a whisper, her eyes flashing conspiratorially.

'Hardly at all,' replied Wilde, somewhat puzzled at the question.

'Why are you here tonight then?'

'Because I was asked. Just a guest speaker. Is that a problem?'

Granger gave a brief whimsical smile and shook her head. 'No, no, of course not. It's just that Ambrose puzzles me, and I thought you might be able to explain.'

'Explain what exactly?'

'Why he allowed me to be a member of the club. I've just had one book published so far, and although it was well received… well, it is only one book. I am sure there are more worthy writers out there who would be a more obvious choice.'

'New blood, I expect. Such organisations cannot flourish without the injection of fresh talent. It's good to have youth and burgeoning promise on board. Have you not asked him yourself?'

'Oh no, that would never do: pas tout à fait de rigueur. Well, thank you for your honesty, Mr Wilde. Now let's dine.' She turned quickly and headed for her seat at the table, leaving Wilde intrigued by the exchange.

There was a great deal of cross-chat during the meal, complaints about publishers and agents. Discussions about poisons and gossip about other authors were the main topics.

Both Wilde and Kishen studied the faces and demeanour of the diners, each building his own catalogue of impressions. Wilde had to admit to himself that not one of the members of the Murder Club gave any hints of a suspicious nature. They appeared relaxed, at ease with their kind; if there was subterfuge here, he could not see it.

There seemed to be little mention of the death of Anthony Carfax, which suggested to Wilde that the fellow was not much liked and would not be missed as a member of the group. At one point, Jacob Brown did ask De Lacy if there was going to be a replacement member for the Club. 'In due course,' De Lacy replied uneasily. 'We must not seem too hasty. That would be most unseemly. In a month or so's time, perhaps, at our next meeting, we should hold a ballot amongst ourselves.'

'Ah,' said Vivien Dowson, 'I will give my apologies now. I will not be able to attend the next meeting. I shall be off to my seaside cottage again to deal with the latest Inspector Forsyth mystery. I desperately need to create a few more red herrings. My deadline is looming, and I write so much better when I'm down there, away from all the attractions of town.'

Wilde saw that De Lacy stiffened awkwardly at this declaration but the author said nothing in reply; he simply nodded as though he didn't want to discuss the matter further.

After the meal was over, the plates were cleared away, and the brandy glasses filled—all apart from Kishen's. He asked for ginger ale, but it never materialised. De Lacy rose from his chair, glass in hand. 'Ladies and Gentlemen, fellow members of the Murder Club, let us take a moment to pay homage to our dear departed member Anthony Carfax. He will be much missed. (Silent but mostly unenthusiastic nods around the table.) Please raise your glasses in sad remembrance of a fellow mystery writer.'

The rest of the group rose, murmured Carfax's name, and took a drink of brandy before resuming their seats.

'Now, we come to the business of the evening,' continued De Lacy in a more relaxed tone. 'It is my pleasant duty to introduce our guest speaker, Mr Rupert Wilde, a war hero, recipient of the George Cross, and now a successful private investigator, someone who deals with real crimes and real mysteries. We are delighted to welcome him here tonight, to speak to us, to give us a little inside information concerning the work of a real-life detective.'

There was a gentle ripple of applause, and Wilde got to his feet and began speaking without notes. He gave the background to a couple of old cases in which he had been involved and the methods he had used to reach a satisfactory conclusion. As he was nearing the end of his speech, he touched briefly, and to Kishen's estimation, somewhat dangerously, on what he referred to as 'my current investigation.'

'It's a matter where my client's life is being threatened by an unknown correspondent,' he said airily, taking care to glance briefly at Ambrose De Lacy to gauge his reaction to this revelation. The author's eyes flickered nervously, and his fingers twitched. It was clear he wondered and indeed feared how much Wilde was going to reveal about the matter.

'In such cases,' Wilde continued, 'the problem lies in discovering the identity of the unknown author of such missives and the purpose behind the threats they contain. Does he—or she—intend to carry them out, or are they just designed to upset and bring a great deal of unease to the recipient? Unfortunately, one cannot rely on the latter scenario. If there is a genuine threat, then the malcontent has made the task of carrying out the deed more difficult because the proposed victim has been alerted to dangers and is on his guard. He will be more prepared to deal with any unforeseen circumstances. In my current investigation, the victim has employed me to seek out the culprit and expose him. And, by golly, I will.'

'Bravo, sir,' said Jacob Brown, 'And have you in fact found out who this demon scribbler is?'

Wilde gave an intriguing smile. 'Ah, I am not at liberty to reveal that. I do not want to compromise this assignment by being too indiscreet. I can only say that I am confident that I shall bring the whole matter to a satisfactory conclusion and that my client will, in the near future, be able to sleep soundly in their bed at night while the malefactor will fall under the full jurisdiction of the law.'

'Bravo, I say again,' bellowed Brown. 'Perhaps when the dust has settled on this business, you will come again and reveal all the details. It could well be the basis for a damned good thriller.'

'Oh, Jake, my darling, don't tell me that you're not bright enough to come up with your own plots?' said Meg Granger as she lit a black Russian cigarette.

Brown bristled a little at this retort, then his features relaxed into a tight grin. 'Of course, I am, but never look a gift horse in the mouth.'

'There is such a thing as plagiarism as well, Brown, old chap,' observed Professor Watkins, who was obviously happy to join in the ribbing of his plump colleague.

At this point, De Lacy tapped his brandy glass with a knife to gain attention. 'Enough of this joshing. I think the time has come to thank Mr Wilde for his contribution this evening.'

'Hear, hear,' chimed in Vivien Dowson, and rapped on the table as a sign of appreciation. The other members followed suit.

'I thank you,' said Wilde, bowing his head.

Further brandy was poured and drunk, and then the assembled throng gravitated towards the fireplace in small conversational groups. Wilde attached himself to the professor and Meg Granger while Kishen, a little adrift, went over to talk to Vivien Dowson. He began by asking her how she came up with ideas for her plots and also about her desire to seek solitude when writing her novels, but the conversation quickly turned to India. The novelist was keen to hear of life and customs there. 'I've had thoughts of setting one of my whodunits in India,' she said. 'The exotic backdrop would add an extra *je ne sais quoi* to the proceedings.'

Kishen had to tell her that it was many years since he had spent time in his native country. 'I was educated in England, at Rugby and Cambridge so, you see, I have lost touch with so much of my ethnic background. I think of myself as an Englishman now, rather than an Indian.'

'Pity,' said Vivien Dowson, lighting up a cheroot, seeming to lose all interest in her companion, his appeal as a research source having vanished.

As members began to say their goodbyes, Meg Granger approached Wilde and, placing a gentle hand on his arm, directed him to a quiet corner of the room. 'I did enjoy your talk tonight, Mr Wilde….'

'Rupert, please.'

'Rupert. I was wondering if I could come to interview you sometime to…how should I put this… extract more information from you about your work, your modus operandi. For professional purposes, you understand.' Her eyes flashed mischievously as though there were some hidden meaning behind her request.

Rupert grinned. 'I am not sure I can really say more than I have tonight. Each case brings with it its own structure and individual demands on how it is approached. There is no template, I'm afraid. I don't have a file labelled 'modus operandi' in my desk drawer.'

'I was thinking maybe if I could sit in on a case, to study it as an outsider.'

Wilde pursed his lips. 'For that, I would need to gain permission from my client. I feel that is unlikely. Most people who approach me for my professional services demand absolute discretion. I am a private detective, with the emphasis on 'private.'

'Pity,' responded the lady. 'I was particularly interested in the threatening letter case you mentioned. Is there no way I could find out more?'

Wilde shook his head. 'I am afraid not. This is not only a delicate matter but a dangerous one. Perhaps when the case is concluded, with the permission of my client, I could tell you more.'

'I understand,' she said with muted disappointment. 'You see, I strive for realism in my stories. I eliminate the romantic and melodramatic elements found in so many crime novels. I want to insert truth and unsettling reality into the narrative. I believe that is the way the future of crime fiction lies.'

'Well, I'm no expert, but what you say makes sense to me. I wish you well with your endeavours.'

'Thank you,' she said before turning swiftly and making her way to the door.

'Well,' said Rupert Wilde as they journeyed by taxi back home, 'I don't think tonight's little jamboree has added much to our stock of useful information regarding this case. It was good to put faces to names and catch a little of their characters, but if there was someone capable of actual murder in the room, they hid that trait excellently.'

'It was as though they were all putting on a performance,' observed Kishen.

'Exactly,' agreed Wilde. 'Whether they do this naturally to keep a protective shell around themselves or if it was for our benefit, I'm not sure. However, I am sure, for instance that Jacob Brown was almost like a pantomime character presenting himself as a bumptious idiot. You can't hide a keen intelligence in the eyes, however much artifice you put into your act. I am sure he is a sharp fellow. Indeed, they all are.'

Kishen nodded. 'Certainly, I thought that the Dowson lady was pretending for a time to be interested in me, but she soon became bored and dropped her mask. What did you make of the two other women?'

'Ah, yes, both very interesting. Meg Granger's behaviour was a little erratic. She took me to one side and seemed particularly interested in finding out more about De Lacy.'

'Oh, really?'

'Of course, that may well be because she feels insecure about being a member of the club. She is the youngest and has had only one novel published.'

'Well, you certainly could not accuse Briony Lodge of being insecure. She was oozing self-confidence.'

'Was she?' mused Wilde. 'I really thought that was a front, covering up a certain nervousness.'

'Nervousness… about what?'

'Ah, that I can't say.'

'Well, that only leaves Professor Alan Watkins….'

'Watkins was certainly playing the slightly absent-minded academic who has just sort of stumbled into the world of crime writing. From his demeanour I really got the impression that he saw himself as somewhat superior to his literary colleagues.' Wilde paused for a moment to light a cigarette. 'Having said all that and carried out a simple analysis of our cast, I don't think we are much nearer to being able to point an accusing finger at any of them.

'Indeed,' agreed Kishen. 'And if any one of them had received a threatening letter like Mr De Lacy's, they certainly didn't react when you mentioned those unsettling missives.'

'Cunning, determined murderers rarely give their game away. Unfortunately for us, they are very good at hiding their true emotions,' Wilde observed with a sigh.

Chapter Twenty-One

T he next morning, after a light, leisurely breakfast, Wilde and Kishen set off for Somerset House, situated on the south side of the Strand, overlooking the river Thames. Since 1837 the north wing of this impressive Neo-Classical edifice has held records of all births, marriages, and deaths in the United Kingdom. It was here that the two men hoped to unearth more details about the Collins family and in particular, Daniel.

Once inside and having filled in the forms required of them to gain access to the files, the two men split up and began their research. It was a long tedious process and was quite some time before either of them discovered any information that could possibly be of use to them. Eventually, after several hours working separately, turning the pages of numerous ledgers, they both reached the conclusion that they had squeezed this particular lemon dry.

'Let's grab a bite of lunch in some nearby hostelry and assemble what jolly old info we've managed to scoop up, scant though it be,' suggested Wilde.

Kishen nodded in agreement.

The Saracen's Head provided them with a ham sandwich and a glass of porter for Wilde and a cheese sandwich and a lemonade for Kishen.

'Vitals first and then chat,' said Wilde.

When the food was consumed, Wilde lit a cigarette and consulted his notes. 'It would appear the Collins family were a fairly well-to-do lot. The father, Harold, was born in 1857. He was a career diplomat, a backroom boy, but nevertheless was awarded the OBE for his pains. From what scant detail I could unearth, he seemed a very decent fellow'.

Kishen flipped the pages of his notebook. 'Examining the marriage certificate, it seems the mother was a Mildred Waite. The occupation given was couturier. They were married in the church of St Monica on the Edgware Road in 1885. That led me on to searching for the death certificates. They actually died on the same day, 15ᵗʰ June 1910. It was a fatal car crash'.

'So, a dead end... in more ways than one', said Wilde. 'I discovered that there were three children. Two boys and a girl. The girl was the eldest, Susan, and then came Wilfred and finally Daniel in 1894.'

Kishen made a note.

'Interesting facts,' observed Wilde, 'but we are without sturdy crampons scaling this mystery mountain. I'm not sure how we get to the next ledge'.

'I have an idea,' said Kishen, tentatively.

'Do you, old lad? Spill the beans....'

Kishen flipped back some pages of his notebook, his finger hovering over his scribbles. 'The best man at the Collins' wedding was Henry Bullivant. According to the records, it would seem that the fellow is still alive. Certainly, his death has not been recorded. If we managed to get in touch with him, maybe he could give us some further information regarding the Collins offspring.'

'Brilliant!' Wilde slapped Kishen on the back. 'The old brainbox is fully charged and working on full power today.' And then his smile faded. '*If* the blighter is still alive, as you say. If he was a contemporary of Harold Collins, which we must assume, he'll be about sixty-five or so now.'

'Not a great age....'

'Quite. Look, there's a telephone booth over there at the back of the room. There must be a directory inside. Let's cast an eye over it and see if the old boy is contactable on the blower. There can't be many Bullivants in there.'

As it turned out there were five in the London area, but only two with the initial H. Wilde and Kishen squeezed into the telephone booth, coins were slotted and the first contact made. This H. Bullivant turned out to be Hilda and a spinster. Wilde chuckled as he replaced the receiver. 'I think we can count her out'. The second call bore fruit. A rasping, somewhat elderly voice responded with the rather haughty announcement, 'Mr Bullivant's residence.'

'May I speak to Mr Bullivant,' said Wilde.

'I'm afraid not,' came the reply. 'The master is taking his noontime nap. He cannot be disturbed.'

'Then I would like to call and speak with your master. It is regarding a matter of great personal importance. I am Major Rupert Wilde GC.'

There was a hissing pause. 'I see. Well...Mr Bullivant has a light lunch at 1.30. Perhaps if you call at three this afternoon, a meeting may be acceptable. I will certainly pass on your message when the master awakes'.

Wilde took note of the address: Bankfield House, 14 Gramercy Road, Regents Park. 'Come, Watson,' he grinned, replacing the receiver and slapping his companion on the back. 'The game's afoot!'

Bankfield House was part of a Georgian terrace situated at the end of a row of similar smart properties. Having rung the bell, Wilde and Kishen had not long to wait. The door was opened by a tall white-haired man, whose height was rather curtailed by his stoop. Before he opened his mouth, Wilde was sure that this was the owner of the voice he had spoken to on the telephone, the one who had referred to Henry Bullivant as 'master'.

He raised a wispy eyebrow. 'Is it Mr Wilde? he said, gazing over Rupert's shoulder at Kishen.

'It is indeed, along with my business associate Mr Chabra.'

'I see....'

'I trust that Mr Bullivant has agreed to see us.'

'Well, I gave him your message, but I understood this was just a meeting between you and him and not... another person.'

'Ah, Mr Chabra is closely linked to the matter I wish to discuss with your master.'

'I see. Very well. Mr Bullivant has agreed to grant you an audience, but I beg that you will be brief as possible. He is not in the best of health and easily gets tired.'

Wilde gave a nod of understanding. 'We shall be as brief as possible.'

They were shown into a large sitting room where most of the blinds were drawn low so that only a small amount of light was able to enter the room. There was a roaring fire in the grate, which filled the chamber with a fierce oppressive heat. Seated by the hearth in a wheelchair was a thin bald-headed man who wore thick horn-rimmed glasses, which were perched precariously on the end of his narrow nose. An open book lay on his lap.

'Major Wilde and his associate Mr Chabra,' announced the butler and then silently withdrew.

Bullivant removed his glasses and gazed at his visitors. 'Welcome, gentlemen. Do take a seat,' he said in a surprisingly strong voice. They did as they were bidden. 'I have few callers these days. My old acquaintances are either dead or incapacitated as I am. It's the way of the world, I suppose. We flourish while we are young, and when we grow old, we fade into the shadows and become invisible. Major, eh? Did you have a good war?'

'If I'm honest, sir, no one had a good war, but I survived.'

Bullivant gave a throaty chuckle. 'A sensible answer. I like it. I must admit, Major, when Johnson, my man, told me of your request to see me on a personal matter, it intrigued me. What's it all about?'

'I will be honest with you, sir. I am a private detective and I am seeking information concerning the family of an old friend of yours: Harold Collins.'

Bullivant's rheumy eyes widened. 'Harold. Heavens, the poor devil has been dead for over ten years.'

'I know. A terrible accident….'

'Terrible indeed.'

'It is his children I am concerned with. I thought you could tell me something about them. I am particularly interested in Daniel.'

'Ah, the children. A funny bunch.'

'In what way, a funny bunch?'

'Well, they certainly weren't a chip off the old block, I can tell you that. Good old Harold was as straight as a die, clear-headed, and bright as a button. Those children were all a little odd. I have to think they got that strain from their mother, Milly. Lovely woman in many ways, bit a little bit…how can I put this… a little bit wayward in her thinking. Not terribly strong mentally, if you catch my drift. Suffered from bouts of depression, poor dear.'

106

'How did this impinge upon the children's character?'

Bullivant gave a dark, ironic laugh. 'I'm not a psychiatrist or a mind doctor. I can only pass on my layman's views and observations.'.

'Those would be most welcome.'

'Very well. But first, if one of you gentlemen would do me the favour of pouring me a large whisky....' He indicated the drinks trolley in the corner of the room. 'I am not allowed strong drink—doctor's orders—and old Johnson, bless him, adheres to these restrictions most assiduously. I know he cares about my health, but if I've not got long to live, I might as well have a little fun in the time left.'

'I will do the dirty deed,' said Kishen lightly with a nod of the head.

''Thank you, and do pour a couple of glasses for yourself and the Major.'

'I do not drink, sir, but I am aware that the Major tends to make up for my deficiency in this area.'

Bullivant laughed. 'Then give him a big one,' he said, grinning.

Once he was nursing the whisky glass between his gnarled fingers, Bullivant gazed at Wilde intently. 'So, you want to know about old Harold's brood, eh?'

Wilde nodded. 'Well, the girl was the first: Susan. She was a handful from the start. A lanky strip of trouble, causing chaos as soon as she could walk. She was sent away to private school, but that didn't seem to do much good—she didn't mend her ways. She was expelled. The minx was only about twelve when she set fire to the dining room curtains—by accident because she was drunk.'

'Drunk at twelve?'

Bullivant gave a wry smile. 'I said she was a handful, precocious, too. Very early on developed a love of champagne and quaffed it like a trooper. Later, in her early teens, she was arrested for shoplifting, and then at eighteen, she got into a fight with another girl and blinded her in one eye. Terrible business. She went to gaol for six months and then disappeared.'

'Disappeared?'

'Yes. When her father went to collect her after she had served her term, she had signed herself out, and, as far as the parents were concerned, they never heard from her again. It was rumoured that she spent some time in a mental institution and then moved abroad to the colonies. Whether all that was just gossip, I'm not sure. I've no idea if she kept in touch with her siblings. I suspect she'll be dead now. With her mentality and temper there wasn't a long life in prospect for such a creature. It's very sad.'

Bullivant took a gulp of whisky. 'Good stuff, this. An Islay single malt.'

'And then there was Wilfred,' prompted Wilde.

'Yes, yes, indeed. Quite the opposite of Susan. Introverted, shy and very much a loner. He had difficulty communicating with people, even his own parents. And easily upset by the simplest of things. I once saw him in floods of tears because he'd mislaid one of his books.' Bullivant shook his head sadly. 'Strange boy. But he had a keen mind and did well at school. He was in the first wave of lads sent out to France in '14. Battle fodder. I gather he had a nervous breakdown in the trenches and was sent home. I know no more about him. I am afraid that after Harold and Milly's death, I had little to do with the family—well, nothing really.'

'And what about Daniel?' asked Kishen.

'Ah, young Daniel. Well, he was perhaps, in one sense, the most normal of them all. Bright, personable, and good-looking. With just one chink in his armour.'

'Chink? What was that?' asked Wilde, guessing already what the answer would be.

Bullivant took another sip of whisky and rolled the liquor around in his mouth before replying. 'How should I put this,' he said at length. 'He had, shall we say, a predilection for individuals of his own gender, if you get my drift.'

Wilde nodded. 'Where is he now?'

Bullivant shrugged. 'No idea. As far as I know, he attended university, and I expect he went over to France to fight those dreadful Germans, but I really am not sure whether that is the case or not. Sorry I cannot be more help.'

'Oh, but you have been a great help. You've filled in a few blanks in the jigsaw puzzle for which we are both grateful.'

'Really?' Bullivant raised a fuzzy eyebrow. 'And may I say you have helped me while away a little time in civilised company with a glass of the prohibited brew. As I observed earlier, I don't get many visitors these days, and Johnson, splendid chap that he is, is lacking in the conversation stakes, I'm afraid.'

Wilde rose and held out his hand. 'I appreciate your time, sir. I wish you well. I am sure a nip of the hard stuff now and then will not do you any harm.'

Bullivant gave a little chuckle and sat back in his chair, his eyelids already fluttering in preparation for a nap.

Wilde and Kishen left the old boy to his slumbers.

Chapter Twenty-Two

On returning home from work, Sally found a large bouquet of flowers waiting for her and a card signed 'affectionally yours, Rupert.' The note also suggested another assignation that evening. 'I will send my assistant to pick you up in a taxi and bring you to my place for a light supper around 8pm. Hope you can make it.'

Sally's spirits rose as she read the note. She was thrilled to think that she would be in the company of that delightful man once more. She held the flowers close to her face and breathed in deeply with a sigh.

It was nearly ten o'clock when Wilde and Kishen made their way home. After their visit to Henry Bullivant, they had taken a long leisurely dinner over which they discussed the case and what they had learned that day. In this way, Wilde was able to document in his mind the various threads, which he hoped very soon he would be able to weave into something significant. There was a surprise waiting for them on their return to the flat. There on the doormat was a foolscap envelope bearing his name scrawled in dark purple ink. The quality of the stationery and the handwriting were identical to those missives received by Ambrose De Lacy.

'What now?' he muttered, picking up the envelope, a feeling of unease growing swiftly within him.

When Sally woke, she was in the dark and lying on a bed. Despite her mind being very woozy, it did not take her long to realise that her hands and feet were bound. With an effort, she attempted to pull herself up into a sitting position. While doing so, she tried to quell the growing sense of panic welling up inside her. She tried to rationalise how she had found herself in this perilous position. She remembered being picked up by a strange individual calling himself Jonathan. He was a tall individual who wore a slouch hat and had a scarf wrapped around the lower part of his face. He called at the house as arranged and announced that he was Rupert's assistant and he was taking her to his flat. He spoke in a strange gruff voice tinged with some kind of accent that she was unable to identify. He led her to a motor car waiting by the kerb. He opened the rear door and she entered, but then as she took her seat…. She gasped at the recollection, the image of the large white pad looming before her face and then it being clamped to her mouth. For a moment, she was so shocked she could not move, and then as she started to struggle, the chloroform began to work, and a misty darkness was growing in her brain. It was only seconds before she slumped forward unconscious.

Now, as she regained her full sensibilities, she realised that she had been drugged and kidnapped! And that man, that Jonathan, had nothing to do with Rupert. She had been tricked. But why? What for? What on earth was all this about? Her puzzlement regarding her predicament overrode any feelings of fear that were waiting in the dark corners of her mind ready to flourish. She was too sensible, too resilient to give in to panic. Not yet, anyway.

Having pulled herself up into a half-sitting position, she began tugging at the rope that bound her wrists, but her efforts were to no avail. The bonds proved incalcitrant. She took a deep breath. She must not cry, she told herself. She must keep as calm and rational as possible. Tears were futile. Allowing her emotions to take over would do no good at all. That, of course, she told herself, was easier said than done.

Bracing herself, she called out with a cry of 'Help.' The word reverberated in the darkened room. She repeated her cry, and this time, in response, there was the sound of a key turning in a lock. This was followed by a broad yellow shaft of light that spilled into the darkness. A tall silhouette materialised in this strip of brightness. It was the person who called himself Jonathan. He

111

still wore the hat and scarf so that his features could not be seen, only the large staring eyes.

'Ah, Sleeping Beauty has awakened,' he said in a harsh whisper as though he was disguising his real voice. Who was he—this creature who had claimed to be an associate of Rupert Wilde, the man who had drugged her, the man who had her completely in his power? At this latter thought, a leak in her resolve appeared, and suddenly Sally gave a little whimper. What did he intend to do with her?

As the man came nearer to the bed, she stifled a cry. She had to be brave, she told herself. Becoming a weeping wreck was not going to help matters.

'There is no need to fear,' the Jonathan character said softly. It was spoken so nonchalantly as though he was passing the time of day. The incongruity of his tone actually increased Sally's fear.

'What do you want with me? Why have you treated me like this? Let me go.'

'Rest assured I will let you go... unharmed, but not until you have served your purpose.'

'My purpose.'

'As bait, my dear. Pretty, vulnerable bait.' The figure took a step nearer the bed and held up his gloved right hand, which held a large pair of scissors.

It was at this point that Sally screamed.

Wilde slit open the envelope and withdrew the sheet of paper inside. It contained a message written in an unfamiliar hand:

Good evening, Mr Wilde

If you wish to see your lovely friend Sally again, you must obey these instructions: Come to the following address at midnight: 23 Glink Street, down by the river in Southwark. Come alone and unarmed. Any trickery on your part will mean the certain demise of the charming Sally. You will recognise her hair here enclosed...

See you at the witching hour.

Wilde glanced inside the envelope and saw a small clutch of blonde hairs. His heart skipped a beat. No doubt they were Sally's. He stared at the note once more with a mixture of horror and anger. He knew that he could not have foreseen this situation, but he felt it was his fault that Sally was now in grave danger. He had no doubt about this. Her life was in peril.

Without comment, he passed the note to Kishen, who, on reading it, gave out a cry of surprise.

'Goodness. This is terrible,' he said. 'What... what do you intend to do?'

Wilde gave a weary shrug of the shoulders. 'Obey my instructions. There is little else I can do.'

'But that will put you in a very vulnerable position.'

'No more vulnerable than Sally's.'

Kishen shook his head. 'What on earth is all this about? I thought the murderer was keen to kill De Lacy.'

'I am sure that they still are, but they want me out of the way first.'

'But why?'

'One can only assume our adversary fears that my investigations on behalf of De Lacy will lead me to discovering their identity. They feel threatened and so want to eliminate that possibility....'

'By eliminating you.'

'That's how it appears to me,' said Wilde with chagrin.

'If you are going to this address, I will come, too.'

Wilde shook his head. 'Oh, no, you don't. You read what the fellow wrote: 'come alone'. I don't want you to end up in the morgue for keeping me company.'

Kishen looked shocked at this statement, but Wilde chuckled and patted his friend's arm. 'I'm not being serious. I certainly don't intend to allow myself to be killed in this venture, but I have to go alone. I must concentrate on looking after Sally. Having someone else with me would only complicate matters and put both our lives at risk.'

'Very well,' said Kishen with a reluctant sigh. 'You know best.'

'Not always, but in this instance....' Wilde suddenly consulted his pocket watch. 'By Jove, it's nearly eleven. I don't have much time to find this wretched address before midnight. Grab me the map of London, would you? I just need to collect something from the kitchen.'

Kishen did as requested. On being presented with the map book, Wilde consulted the street index and then flipped through the pages to locate Glink Street.

'As I thought,' he murmured. 'Not a very salubrious area.' He glanced at his watch again. 'I better scoot. I'll take the roadster....'

'I could drive you.'

'What did I say about going on my own...?'

'Just a thought.'

'A kind but an ill-conceived one. Hold the fort until I get back.'

As Kishen heard the front door bang, a dark cloud of despair seemed to settle on him. 'I reckon that tonight I should offer up a few prayers,' he said to himself. And then some lines of Shakespeare flashed into his mind:

'Good things of day begin to droop and drowse,

Whiles nights black agents to their prey do rouse.'

At the recollection of these words, Kishen gave a deep involuntary shudder.

Chapter Twenty-Three

It did not take Wilde long to locate Glink Street, which was situated south of the river in an area dominated by lofty warehouses, some of them now derelict after the war. There were a few dilapidated dwelling houses down near the water's edge and it was to one of these that he made his way. None of them offered up any signs of habitation. He visualised his enemy holed up in one of them, holding Sally hostage, awaiting his arrival with a gun or some other weapon ready to kill him. This must not happen nor Sally come to any harm. But how he was to achieve this he had no real notion. He was now acting purely on adrenalin and instinct.

Keeping to the moonlight shadows, he edged his way down the sloping cobbled street until he came to number 21, the property next door to his destination. As he gazed up at the building, a stream of rats emerged from out of the dark and scurried across the street, disappearing into the inky blackness beyond. Number 23 was silent with not a flicker of light about the place. Instinctively he touched the bottom of his right trouser leg and felt the comforting shape of the small kitchen knife that he had slipped down his sock before leaving his apartment. His emergency weapon.

Across the city, he heard the mournful chimes of Big Ben announcing the hour of midnight. Slowly he edged his way to the door of 23 and to his surprise it was slightly ajar. This had all the hallmarks of an obvious trap, but what choice did he have? Slipping inside, his nose was assailed with the powerful odour of damp, rot, and decay, clearly telling Wilde that the property had not been lived in for some time. The two large rooms on the ground floor and a decrepit scullery kitchen were dark, empty, and silent.

Making his way to the foot of the staircase, he held still, straining his ears for any slight sound that may indicate where his tormentor was located.

There was nothing. The air hissed with silence. So quiet was it that Wilde believed he could easily be convinced that he had suddenly gone deaf. Then the thought struck him; maybe this was a wild goose chase. The bounder was playing games with him. There really was no one here. Just as this idea began to take shape and grow in his mind, he heard a sound. It was so faint at first that he was not sure whether he had imagined it. But it came again, slightly louder. It was a whimper, a sob, gentle but real, floating on the damp tainted air. This was gentle exhalation of grief from someone who was in distress and it came from the upper floor.

There it was again. More guttural and elongated this time. It had to be Sally, he thought. She must be a prisoner in one of the bedrooms. A prisoner trussed up like a Christmas turkey, no doubt with her gaoler waiting for him to rush in and rescue her, waiting with a gun to blast him to kingdom come.

With gritted teeth, he began to ascend the stairs. He moved as stealthily as he could, desperately trying to avoid the assorted debris lying beneath his feet. His progress was painfully slow but he managed to maintain his silence.

At last, he reached the landing and stood once more for some time just listening. The sobs had ceased, and he was unsure which direction to take. His eyes had by now become acclimatised to the darkness, and he was able to make out the geography of his surroundings. In the broad corridor before him, there were two doors to his right and another door to his left, each, he assumed, was a bedroom. The distressed sobbing must have come from one of these rooms. But which? He gazed around him, searching the shadows for signs of another presence on the landing. There was none.

He had a vision of his enemy standing flat against the wall behind one of these doors, waiting for him to enter, ready to club him, stab him, or shoot him.

Bending down he picked up a stray piece of wood and threw it down the corridor where it landed with a gentle thump. The sound broke the silence and prompted a plaintive cry from the room at the far end of the corridor on the right. That was where she was and, no doubt, that was where his protagonist was also.

With infinite slowness, Wilde moved towards the room. As he grew nearer, he was able to see a thin line of pale amber light running down the side of the door. It was time for action. Now he was calm. All his army training came into play. He had been in many a tight spot during the war. This, he told himself, was another such occasion. He must tackle it with a cool head and sharp mind and he must survive.

Taking a deep breath, he thrust the door open with enough force to push it back hard against the wall. It crashed noisily, the sound echoing loudly around the building. It was followed by silence. There was certainly no one there waiting to ambush him. In carrying out this action, he had dropped down into a crouch and then slowly moved forward into the room. It was dimly lighted by one candle. The only furniture was an old bed. Lying on the bed was Sally, hunched up against the bedhead in a sitting position. She was bound and gagged. Wilde rose to his feet, his eyes sweeping the room, searching for another presence but apart from the girl there was no one there.

Pulling the knife out, he rushed to the bed and cut through Sally's bonds. She fell sobbing into his arms. He held her tight briefly, allowing her time to control her emotions. Slowly the tremors faded, and her breathing eased.

'Cheer up, old girl. It's all over. You're safe now,' he said softly.

'Oh, Rupert, it's been a nightmare.'

'Are you injured? Did the devil hurt you?'

She shook her head, tears still streaming down her face. 'No, no. He drugged me and cut my hair. It was horrible. I was so frightened. Where is he now?'

Wilde shook his head. 'I don't know. The main thing is to get you out of here and to somewhere safe. Are you strong enough to walk?'

'Yes, yes, I think so.' She brushed her sleeve across her face, drying her eyes.

Putting his arm around Sally, Wilde pulled her to the edge of the bed. 'See if you can stand.'

With his help, Sally gradually edged herself off the bed into an upright position. She wavered for a moment and then sat back down on the mattress. 'I'm sorry,' she said. 'I feel a little weak, but let's try again.'

On the second attempt, with his support, she was able to stand and take a few steps forward. Despite everything, she managed a smile.

'Good girl,' he said warmly, returning the smile.

As they moved forward a few steps, Wilde stopped suddenly. He saw that the door that he had so dramatically and violently smashed against the wall was now closed. Someone had pulled it to. Again, he glanced around the room to see if there was someone lurking in the shadows. There was no one. But the door had not closed of its own volition. As he tried to turn the handle to open it, he discovered that it was locked.

'What is it?' asked Sally, not fully aware of the situation.

'It seems we have been locked in,' said Wilde, helping her back to the bed. 'Sit there while I see to it. A little brute force should settle the matter.'

Initially, he hurled himself against the door with as much force as he could muster, but it was a stout recalcitrant beast and failed to submit to his assault. He tried once more with a similar result. Then he tried a different approach. Lifting his leg high, he thrust it hard against the lock. 'Open sesame!' he cried as he did so. This time the door shook, and the wood around the lock showed faint signs of splintering. Two more attempts and the door began to surrender. One final assault on the lock and the door finally gave way, and he was able to wrench it open. The sight that met his eyes froze him on the spot. The landing was alight. Hungry red flames were in the process of devouring the passageway. So that was it, Wilde thought, his mind grasping the perilous situation in a trice. That was the nature of the trap. To lure him to a locked room at the top of the building and then set the place on fire.

He ran to the bed and pulled Sally to him. 'We have to get out of here pronto, old thing.'

Her eyes widened with horror as she caught sight of the flames. Wilde stripped off his overcoat and wrapped it around Sally, pulling it over her head.

'This is to protect you. We have to get out of here without delay, so I'm going to give you a fireman's lift. Just make sure you have covered all your vulnerable flesh with the material of my coat. Do you understand?'

She nodded, the terror never leaving her eyes. 'Yes...' came the faint reply.

'Good. I've got to try and get us to the staircase. Now get ready for the lift.'

Lowering his frame, Rupert Wilde hauled Sally over his shoulder and then made his way at speed out of the room. A wave of heat swept over him as he moved into the corridor. At present, the flames were hungrily climbing up the walls but were still allowing a narrow path between the two sides. Keeping his head down, he hurried along the corridor towards the landing. As he did so, eager flames flicked out towards him as though they had sensed his flight and were determined to stop it. At the top of the stairs, he looked down into the well of the house. It was an inferno of bright red and orange. The heat and the thick grey clouds of suffocating, noxious fumes rolled up to envelop him. There was no hope of escape down the stairs. They would be roasted alive in seconds.

Across the street, Wilde's nemesis stood in the shadows, smoking a cigarette and smiling as they saw the fire take hold of the old building, which had succumbed easily to the power of the flames. The stranger smiled broadly. This had been a successful venture. They had certainly put paid to the interfering activities of a certain Rupert Wilde. No one could survive such an inferno. Now they could return to the main mission of terrifying and then eliminating that snake in the grass, Ambrose De Lacy. With a satisfied smirk, the stranger threw the cigarette into the gutter and then made their way up the street, leaving the building across the road to be consumed by fire.

Frantically, Wilde looked around him for some way of escaping the encroaching flames. They certainly could not return to the far room. A curtain of flame was barring the way. There was nothing... unless... Instinctively, he moved to the door of the first bedroom, and pushing it open, he entered, with Sally still lying heavy and silent across his shoulder. The room was bigger than the one in which he had discovered Sally. It had two distinct advantages: the fire had not reached here yet, and there was a large window at the rear of the room.

'Listen, Sally,' he called over the roar of the fire. 'I'm going to put you down. Okay?'

He received a muffled response which he assumed was in the positive.

Once she was standing, Sally let Wilde's coat settle on her shoulders. She was too shocked by the events to make any comment. Wilde pulled away the grating from the fireplace and began smashing the glass in the window with it. Once he had cleared the aperture, he peered out, breathing in the clean cold night air. There was a twelve foot drop to the garden below. However, just situated to the left of the window, there was a little garden shed which was only about eight feet down.

With less than gentlemanly finesse, he dragged Sally over to the window. 'Sorry, my dear, but you've got to be awfully brave. The only way out is through this window and down'.

'Down!' This was a gasp of horror as she stared out into the darkness beyond the room.

'Yes. It will be tricky, but you can do it. We have no other alternative.' In a calm and as steady a voice as he could muster, in brisk hurried tones, he explained what, with his help, she had to do.

She said nothing, still partially drugged, her face devoid of any emotion, as though the dark spiral of events was robbing her of a foothold in reality, but nevertheless, she gave Wilde an affirmative nod.

Already the fire was beginning to make its presence felt in the room. The door was being consumed by flames, yellow fingers of which were now slowly advancing across the floor. Wilde helped her to clamber up to the windowsill, noting with some anxiety that she was still unsteady on her feet and then, clamping his hands firmly around Sally's wrists, he helped to edge her way out of the window before lowering her down gently so that she was hanging, swinging like some enormous pendulum.

'Are you ready, Sally?' Wilde called, leaning as far out of the window as he dared, allowing Sally to move further down the outside wall. 'I'll swing you more to increase your momentum, and then when I give you the word, I'll let go, and you must leap to the top of the hut to your left. It is less than a three-foot drop.'

Sally's pale face gazed up at him, her eyes filled with a mixture of apprehension and what Wilde perceived as a steely kind of determination.

Wilde knew that if his estimations were wrong, it could be fatal for Sally, but with the sheet of fire at his back, there really was no alternative. Here goes, he thought, as he swung Sally a little harder and then gave the cry, 'Now!' At the same time, he released his grip on her wrists. She sailed sideways and, for a moment, was airborne before dropping down on to the edge of the hut. She gave a moan of pain as her body began to slither over the edge. She squirmed vigorously and managed to pull herself forward.

'Well done, Sally,' he muttered to himself as he clambered out of the window and slipped down the wall while holding the stone of the window sill. Now it was his turn to sway and project himself towards the hut. He landed awkwardly and rolled over the edge. Miraculously, he managed to grab hold of the guttering with one hand. Sally shuffled forward to offer him help, but he realised she wouldn't have the strength to pull him up, but really there was no problem now. Dangling as he was from the roof of the hut, he was less than eight feet from the ground. He simply had to let himself drop down, preparing himself for the jolt when his feet hit terra firma. Flexing his body as he had been trained to do in the army, he landed effectively. With knees bent, he curled his body into a forward roll. As he pulled himself to his feet, he could not help smiling and emitting a little laugh. It was a release of tension after the life-threatening scenario he had just endured. But it wasn't all over yet. He had to help Sally down from the roof of the hut.

'Are you okay up there?' he asked almost flippantly, the smile still on his lips.

'I think so,' came the reply. 'But I'll be a lot happier when I'm down there with you.'

'No sooner said than done. You slip over the edge, dangle down and when I tell you—let go. And I'll catch you.'

Sally obeyed his instructions, and in less than a minute, she was standing close to him, and he was giving her a big hug.

'Can…can we get away from here, please?' she said. There was still a tremor of fear in her voice.

'Of course. My car is not far away.'

Taking her hand, Wilde led her round the building and up the street towards his car. Behind them, the conflagration had now completely taken hold of 23 Glink Street, creating a false yellow dawn to the surrounding area.

Wilde drove them back to his apartment. They travelled in silence. The dramatic experience they had just undergone had robbed them of speech. In Wilde's case, his mind was awash with thoughts and concerns. He knew that he now had to work out how he was going to tackle the rest of this case and, more importantly, make certain that neither he nor Sally were placed in such a life-threatening situation again. He cast a furtive glance in her direction. Her face, illuminated by the lights of the dashboard, was expressionless. She stared ahead of her, but it was clear that she was not really seeing the road ahead. The dear girl was lost in deep thought, still partially drugged, and in some state of shock. No doubt, Wilde thought, she was coming to terms with the fact that she had been very close to losing her life that night.

Chapter Twenty-Four

Despite the lateness of the hour, they found Kishen was still up awaiting Wilde's return. Gazing at the dishevelled and grubby pair, his eyes widened in shock.

'This is Sally,' Wilde said, offering no word of explanation regarding their ragged appearance.

Kishen nodded awkwardly, but he eventually found his voice. 'Pleased to meet you.' He held out his hand, and she took it in a gentle shake.

'And you, Kishen,' said Sally with a smile.

Wilde could not help giving a suppressed chuckle at this ridiculous formality coming at the tail end of such a dramatic evening.

'What on earth has happened?' asked Kishen, confounded by this strange turn of events. Here was his boss, scruffy and tattered and reeking of smoke, with his young lady friend who looked as though she had been crying after being pulled through a hedge backwards.

'Later, old boy. At the moment, I reckon we could do with some vitals—bacon and eggs will do, if you don't mind. And Sally would no doubt like to clean herself up.'

'Yes, please,' she said eagerly.

While she went off to the bathroom and Kishen busied himself in the kitchen preparing the food, Wilde poured himself a large scotch and downed it swiftly in one go. Then, with a deep sigh, he sat down as the alcohol eased the tension in his body. Another shot of scotch and his brain began to function more effectively, and very slowly, a plan began to form in his mind.

It wasn't long before Sally emerged from the bathroom. She had washed her face, combed her hair, and sponged down some of the stains on her dress. 'I feel a little more human now,' she said with a smile. Wilde believed that anyone giving her a passing glance would never guess that she had undergone a series of traumatic events that night. What a remarkable girl, he thought.

'You look eminently presentable, my dear. Come sit down by me. A late supper will be served shortly.'

Sally gave a little frown. 'I really need to contact my father. He will be very worried. I must put his mind at rest.'

'Of course. There is a telephone in my study. You can make a private call from there. You'd better say you are staying with friends tonight.'

When Sally emerged from the study some five minutes later, Kishen had delivered the bacon and eggs with two large mugs of steaming tea. He sat back with a grin of pleasure as Wilde and Sally tucked into the food with gusto.

'So,' said Kishen, after the plates were clean, 'how long are you going to keep me in the dark? What on earth has happened to you tonight?'

Rupert Wilde lit a cigarette and sat back in his chair. 'The story, old lad, is a dramatic one, and the events of this evening prove quite clearly that our adversary, in this case, is a more dangerous, cunning, and ruthless individual than I had given them credit for.'

Kishen nodded eagerly. 'So, tell me all about it,' he said softly, a touch of irritation in his voice at Wilde's prevarications.

Wilde blew a spiral of smoke in the air, did as he was requested and told Kishen 'all about it'. He related the events fully, which enabled him to fix in his own mind all the details of the incident for future reference.

'Great heavens,' exclaimed Kishen, when Wilde had finished. He then turned towards Sally. 'And you are sure you are unhurt, miss?'

'No bones broken,' she replied, 'but it is an experience I have no wish to repeat.'

Kishen nodded. 'I can well understand.'

'Now tell me your story, Sally,' said Wilde patting her arm gently. 'How did you come to end up in that building?'

She recounted how she had received the message purporting to come from Wilde and the strange creature who had called for her and drugged her.

'Did you get a good look at his face?'

Sally shook her head. 'No, he was well muffled up, and I am sure he wasn't using his real voice either. It was artificially guttural. I hope it's a voice I never hear again.'

'And you won't, if I have anything to do with it,' said Wilde grimly.

So, what happens now, Rupert?' asked Kishen. 'How are we to catch this very dangerous villain?'

'As usual, Kishen, you get to the nub of the matter with your question. And it is a fine question but, alas, not an easy one to answer. However, to some extent, events have placed a course of action in our way which I think we should follow. Sally, my dear, what did you say to your father just now?'

'Well, obviously, I didn't tell him the truth. That would have sent his blood pressure sky-high. As you suggested, I told him I was staying with friends tonight. The party I had attended had gone on rather a long time, and I had been offered a bed for the night. He was just relieved to hear my voice and was content with the explanation.'

'That's good. You can certainly have my bed here. I'll camp down on the sofa. That is easily settled, but it's what we do tomorrow that really matters.'

'What do you mean?'

'I am afraid you have now become a very vulnerable pawn in this dangerous game. The individual who kidnapped you did so in order to get at me. They bear you no ill; it's me that they want dead.'

'But why?'

'Because they fear that I will discover their identity. This character is a heartless murderer and has already killed once and is threatening one of my clients.'

'Gracious. How horrible.'

Wilde paused for a moment as though he was rearranging his thoughts. 'One thing in our favour,' he said at length, 'is that our antagonist now believes we are both dead—consumed by the fire they ignited in that derelict building.'

Sally's body gave a gentle shudder as images of the treacherous all-

125

consuming flames flashed into her mind.

'If we continue to let them believe that we perished in that conflagration, it will give me more freedom to carry out my investigations without having to keep looking over my shoulder all the time and also worrying about your safety.'

'Yes, I see the sense of that, but how...?'

'You will have to leave town. Go somewhere safe in the country for a while. Our friend will not think of looking for you. For them, you are now a dead woman. I am their prey. But if you are seen carrying out your normal life... That will give the game away, and we'll both become targets again. Is there somewhere you can stay for a week, or maybe two?'

Sally thought for a moment. 'Well...I have an aunt in Brighton. I have stayed with her before. I suppose...'

'Excellent. That will keep you safe and dry. You can arrange that?'

'I think so. It will mean a few more white lies, I'm afraid.'

'Small concerns when compared to the alternative.'

'What about you? I don't suppose you have an aunt in Brighton.' Sally gave him a cheeky grin.

"Fraid not. Maybe I'll try a beard to disguise the old phizzog. What do you think, Sally? Do you think a set of grey whiskers would suit me?' It was now his turn to flash a cheeky grin.

'I suspect you'd look a bit like an old pirate.'

Wilde laughed. 'Shiver my timbers, you may be right. Still, I'll be okay. If we print an obituary in the press, that should satisfy our enemy—for the time being, at least. I've got to work fast and very astutely, too. This foe is dangerous, and they need to be caught before they can do any more mischief. Well, that's settled. You are off to Brighton, and I shall be lying very low. So, my dear, let me show you to your room. Get as much sleep as you can, and then in the morning, you can make arrangements to have that little holiday by the sea with auntie.'

After Sally had retired for the night, Wilde poured himself another whisky. 'Can't tempt you, I suppose,' he said to Kishen, holding up the bottle.

'Get thee behind me, Satan,' came the light-hearted response. 'As you well know, I am not allowed, but also, I have seen how that stuff can make idiots of sane, intelligent men.'

'Too true. But in moderation, it helps to knit up that ravelled sleeve of care.'

'Like sleep, and I think I am ready for my bed. If you don't mind....'

As Kishen rose from his chair, Wilde held up his hand to stop him. 'Bear with me a mite longer, old boy. There are certain things we have to sort out before the morrow. I have tasks I need you to do, and arrangements need to be made.'

Kishen resumed his seat. 'Of course,' he said easily. 'Tell me more.'

I want you to get on to the *Times* with an obituary notice. Report to them the death of war veteran Rupert Wilde, GC, in a house fire in Southwark. That sort of thing.'

'Gosh, that will upset many people. They will want to attend your funeral.'

'Ah, my dear Kishen, not so many. Apart from you and old Johnny Ferguson, I have no other close friends and no family, of course. If you get enquiries about wanting to see me lowered into the ground in a wooden box, just tell them it is a very private ceremony at my request.'

'Very well. As you wish. It is so sad.'

Wilde leaned forward and patted Kishen on the shoulder. 'It's not real, you know, old boy. I'm not actually dead. I'm still here and intend to remain so. This is only a temporary subterfuge until we have caught our prey in our nets.'

'And what about Ambrose De Lacy?'

Wilde frowned. 'Ah, there we have a problem. I'm not quite sure how we handle him. If he thinks I'm dead and, more particularly, killed by his nemesis, he could go berserk. And yet, if we let him into our secret, he may in some way let the cat out of the bag.'

The two men sat in silence for a few minutes pondering this quandary.

'What if,' Kishen proffered at length, 'we tell him you have gone undercover following an important lead, and it is imperative that the murderer believes you are.... dead?' He gave a gentle shudder. 'Oh, how I hate saying that word.'

Wilde pursed his lips as he mulled over the idea. 'That sounds a reasonable plan. Yes, I think that might work. I'm afraid you'll have to pass this news on to the old feller yourself. It would be dangerous for me to turn up on his doorstep. There is no knowing if his place is being watched.'

Kishen nodded in agreement.

'You must stress that he carries on with his life as normal. Emphasise that he is in no danger...' Wilde paused and gave a sigh, '...despite the fact that he very well may be.'

'He is a difficult customer. He will take some convincing.'

'I know, but I have faith in your powers of persuasion. Unlike me, you are not like the proverbial bull at the gate but rather the gentle snake that carefully slithers under the gap beneath the door.'

Kishen laughed. 'It is not an image that I favour but I will do my best.'

'Ah, you always do.'

'Well, we move into unusual times, but the big question is: do you have a lead, some clue as to what to do next?'

Wilde did not reply; he just poured himself another large whisky.

Chapter Twenty-Five

The following morning, Detective Inspector Johnny Ferguson had a visitor at his office in Scotland Yard. The man who stood before his desk wore dark glasses and a large muffler, which covered the lower region of his face. Ferguson, who was unfazed by this apparition, would have found it difficult to identify the fellow had it not been for the voice, which was rich and refined.

'Sorry to bother you so early,' he said.

'What is this, Rupert? Why the incognito outfit?'

'Ah, I think you have nailed my new soubriquet: Mr Incognito,' replied Wilde pulling off his scarf and slipping the dark glasses into his overcoat pocket.

'Take a seat, Mr Incognito, and tell me what this charade is all about.'

Wilde did as he was bidden and lit a cigarette. 'Well, I have to begin by informing you that I am dead.'

Ferguson raised a cynical eyebrow. 'Well, I have to say you are the healthiest corpse I've ever seen. Come on, cut to the quick - spill the beans.'

And so, Rupert Wilde did in fact spill the beans, the whole steaming panful, while his friend sat mesmerised by the recital.

'Therefore, when I read your obituary in *The Times* tomorrow, I have to resist sending a wreath and my condolences.'

'It would be best,' grinned Wilde.

'I suppose you've come to see me regarding Daniel Collins, that fellow you were keen to locate.'

'Nail driven squarely on the head.'

Ferguson leaned forward and withdrew a manilla file from his desk. He flipped it open and retrieved a single sheet of paper. 'I put my sergeant Bob Sanders onto the job. He's a regular bloodhound. However, I'm afraid he came up with slim pickings. Your chappie Collins disappeared suddenly and without a trace about four years ago. Apparently, he was just about to enrol in officer training before being shipped to France to join the fray there, but he failed the medical. However, it turned out that the man who took the examination was an imposter, a weakling paid by Collins to impersonate him. It was not an uncommon practice. When the truth was discovered, your boy had disappeared. It was thought that he had deliberately joined that invisible troop of men who run to ground rather than face up to their duty to fight for the homeland. From his nosing around, Bradley got the impression that young Daniel was a rather fey and foppish individual, hardly the material for a soldier's role. After that, there seems to be no information regarding what he did next or where he went to. Vanished without a trace. On the other hand, his older brother, Wilfred, did quite badly in the war, suffering a complete breakdown. Poor devil ended up in a mental institution.'

Wilde nodded gently. 'Which institution?'

Ferguson took a closer look at the sheet of paper. 'Brandwell. It's near Oxford.'

'And he's there now?'

Ferguson shrugged. 'One assumes so.'

Wilde rose swiftly. 'Well, thanks, old lad. You've added a new page to my dossier in this case. Whether it will help to bring it to a satisfactory conclusion is something that only time will tell.'

'I hope it helps.'

'Do keep in touch if you have any further info for me. You can pass anything on to Kishen, and he'll get it to me.'

'Will do, and for goodness' sake, watch your back.'

'Of course.'

Ferguson rose and shook his friend's hand. 'Bon chance, *mon ami*,' he said.

'And that's all you can tell me?' Ambrose De Lacy was not a happy man;

his deep frown and anguished voice told Kishen as much. The perturbed author began pacing the floor, shaking his head. 'This is not good enough, you know,' he growled. 'Your master is afraid to visit me—his client—and leaving me in the hands of his manservant.'

'Rupert is not my master, and I am not his manservant.' There was a rare edge of steel to Kishen's response. 'We are colleagues, and I assure you that Mr Wilde is not afraid to visit you. As I told you, he has gone undercover. Any action that he has taken is to assure the best outcome of this investigation.'

'Maybe,' De Lacy responded in a tone that indicated he was not fully convinced by Kishen's words. 'But what is the reason he cannot come here and explain the situation himself?'

'It is simply that it's imperative that the person behind his mischief believes that Rupert is dead. If he is seen visiting you, that fallacy will be exposed. In the meantime, he is following up a very promising lead. I stress that Mr Wilde's actions are in the best interest of the case.'

'Are they? Apparently, they are not in the best interest for me. He has left me vulnerable and exposed.'

'No, no, sir. That is not so. While Mr Wilde has dropped out of public view, he is, as I indicated, still very much on the case and is keeping a very wary eye out for you. And, of course, I am also on hand to help protect you.'

De Lacy rolled his eyes nastily and uttered a disparaging groan. 'And pray tell me, why has Wilde found it necessary to fabricate his own death?'

'In order to put our antagonist off guard.'

'Sounds a somewhat cockeyed idea to me. And in the meantime, what about me? What am I to do while Wilde is lurking in the shadows somewhere?'

'You should carry on as normal. Do not do anything out of the ordinary. If you receive any form of contact from the…' Here, Kishen paused. He didn't want to use the words 'murderer' or 'killer'; they were too brutal and would inflame De Lacy's senses all the more, reminding him of the seriousness of the threat hanging over him. Kishen snatched the least offensive word he could think of and continued. '…miscreant, such as a letter or phone call, just get in touch with us as soon as possible.'

'By which time I could be dead. Why all the cloak and dagger?'

'I assure you it is important in order to bring this dark business to a successful conclusion. You must trust Mr Wilde; he does know best.'

De Lacy gave a heavy sigh and shrugged his shoulders. 'It seems I have little choice in the matter.'

At this point, the telephone rang. Its forceful tones completely unnerving the author. Kishen glanced at the receiver but said nothing. For a moment, De Lacy seemed rooted to the spot, and then he moved awkwardly across the room and, glancing across at Kishen with a worried look, picked up the handset. He clamped it to his ear. As he listened to the speaker at the other end of the line, his eyes widened, and his mouth opened in surprise. 'Yes,' he said at length, his voice barely above a whisper. 'Yes, yes,' he repeated, adding, 'of course. Yes, I understand.'

The line went dead, but De Lacy stood as though frozen, the phone remaining clamped to his ear for some moments. 'That was...that was your Mr Wilde,' he said, finally returning the receiver to its cradle.

Kishen, who was already aware of this, simply smiled.

'He rang to assure me that he was working hard on the case and that... and that my safety was his greatest priority.'

'It was as I told you,' said Kishen with a slight note of smugness. 'I hope that now you are reassured and that Mr Wilde is in no way being neglectful in this matter.'

'I suppose so.' De Lacy sighed and reached for a cigarette from a silver box on the mantelpiece. 'However, I am afraid I will not be at complete ease until this ghastly business is all over.'

Chapter Twenty-Six

The stranger was delighted to see the notification of the death of Rupert Alwyn Wilde in the *Times*. Poor fellow had burnt to death in a mysterious house fire. They smiled with delight on re-reading the brief notification. It was just a pity he simply got in the way, but nothing was going to prevent the stranger in their mission of righting the wrongs. They regarded themselves as an angel of justice in this matter, and their job was nearly complete. Just one other irritant to be dealt with, and then they were ready to take the major prize. Casting the newspaper aside, the stranger lit a cigarette and smiled. Everything was working out just dandy. Poor old De Lacy must be trembling in his shoes now that his knight in shining armour had been eliminated from the lists. 'However, they murmured, 'before I get to you Ambrose, old boy, there is one other player in this sordid drama who I need to deal with first. With their death, one closer to home than Carfax, you will really know the meaning of fear.'

Chapter Twenty-Seven

Brandwell was a large gothic monstrosity with crenelated battlements and ornate towers at either end of its massive structure. It was situated some ten miles from Oxford in a remote area that contained nothing but rolling grassland, punctuated at intervals with small areas of woodland. There were no houses or even, as far as Wilde could determine, farmsteads in the vicinity. Whoever had built this bleak structure had obviously desired isolation. He presumed that it had been a domestic dwelling at some point in its history, a grand house for some wealthy family, but now it was a government possession and had become Brandwell Mental Institution. However, it did not advertise this fact on the stone gateposts; there was just the word Brandwell carved into the granite, which was in danger of being obliterated by time and moss. Below it was a more recent and more utilitarian sign which bore the legend. 'Government Property. No Admittance.' Wilde drove his roadster up to the large rusting gates of the institution, which were closed, and blew his horn. Nothing happened at first. And so, he blew it again. It echoed in the barren surroundings like the bleat of a wounded animal.

Out of nowhere, it seemed, there appeared a man in a blue military-type uniform, with a peaked cap pulled down over his forehead. He was carrying a shotgun. Wilde got out of the car and waved at him in a friendly manner. 'Can't you read?' came the brusque, harsh response.

Ah, he's one of those, thought Wilde. He met quite a few in the army. He moved close to the gates. 'I have an appointment with Dr Mellor,' he said, still retaining his friendly demeanour.

'Have you now?' The man let his grip on the gun relax while he extracted a notepad from the top pocket of his uniform. 'And what's your name?'

'Wilde. Rupert Wilde.'

'Is it now?' came the reply as he scrutinised a page of the notepad. 'You were due here an hour ago.'

'I know. I've travelled from London. The traffic was bad and this isn't the easiest place to find.'

'The traffic was bad...' he repeated Wilde's words with a sneer. 'Well, Mr Rupert Wilde, the whole point of this establishment is that it is not that easy to find. We've got a tinderbox of loonies in here. It's best they are kept well away from us normal folk.'

Wilde raised an eyebrow of disdain at this lack of empathy with his charges and waited.

With some reluctance, the man unlocked the gates and swung them open.

'You are so kind,' observed Wilde with unrestrained sarcasm before slipping back into his car and speeding up the drive towards the house.

Some moments later he was admitted into the building by a large man in a white coat who had questioned him about his visit to Brandwell before he had been allowed to cross the threshold. Wilde noted a small bulge in the pocket of his coat, the shape of which looked very much like the outline of a pistol. Was that, he wondered, for the benefit of the patients or visitors.

The man led him across a large hall, their footsteps echoing eerily in the silence. On reaching a large, impressive door which bore the legend Doctor V. R. Mellor, the man knocked discreetly. A voice from within responded: 'Come.'

'Wait here,' said the man and he slipped into the room. He emerged seconds later. 'You can go in now,' he said before turning on his heel and marching away.

The room was like a Victorian womb: a fire flickered brightly in the grate and the walls were adorned with dark oak panelling. There were large stained-glass windows which gave a strange multi-coloured aura to the surroundings. Two of the walls housed tall bookcases, while over the mantelpiece a large portrait of a stern-looking fellow with impressive mutton chop whiskers glowered down on the chamber.

Seated at an enormous impressive carved desk was a slim woman, with long gaunt features, which were partly hidden by thick horn-rimmed glasses. Her dark hair was pulled back away from her face and tied in a tight bun. Despite the severity of her features, Wilde thought that she was strangely attractive. It was difficult to gauge her age, but he suspected she had not yet reached forty. As he approached, she rose from her chair, and Wilde was surprised at how tall she was—at least six feet, he estimated.

'Mr Wilde,' she said smoothly, extending her hand. Wilde shook it. The grasp was firm and the palm was silky smooth and cold. 'I am Doctor Viola Mellor.' She gave a slight smile. 'My father was a lover of Shakespeare,' she added as an explanation. 'My middle name is Regan.' It was a line, Wilde thought, she used regularly with new acquaintances. 'I am the chief administrator of this institution—as you no doubt are aware.'

'Yes, of course. I am most grateful that you have agreed to see me.'

'Ah, well, when one receives an urgent call from a Detective Inspector from Scotland Yard requesting such an interview, one has little choice. Do take a seat, Mr Wilde, and tell me how I may help you, if that is possible. If we could keep this brief. You are somewhat late for your appointment and I have pressing business to attend to.'

Dr Mellor's tone was pleasant, professional but there was a steely coolness to her voice that clearly indicated to Wilde that this lady was no soft touch and had no appetite for dealing with enquiring strangers. The interview was already sizing up to be a tough one.

'I am requiring information regarding one of your patients, Wilfred Collins. He figures on the periphery of an investigation in which I am currently involved. You know that I am a private detective.'

Dr Mellor nodded. 'Inspector Ferguson informed me as much.'

'I was wondering if I could see Wilfred.'

'That will not be possible.'

Wilde decided to press on. 'It would be of the greatest assistance to me, and it is possible that any information I can secure from such a meeting may help to save a life.'

CHAPTER TWENTY-SEVEN

'As I say, Mr Wilde, that is not possible.'

'Why not?'

'For the simple reason that Wilfred Collins is not here. He is no longer on the premises.'

'You mean he has been moved to another institution.'

With some reluctance, Dr Mellor shook her head. 'I regret to inform you that Wilfred Collins… left Brandwell some three months ago. We have no knowledge of his current whereabouts.'

Vivien Dowson's doorbell tinkled insistently without interval. Someone was eager to see her, she thought, with some irritation. She was desperately trying to finish the current chapter she was working on before beginning to pack ready to leave for her country retreat by the sea. She called out to her daily woman, 'Daisy, see who that is, will you? Unless it's a friend, send them away.' Dowson knew that Daisy was an excellent gatekeeper and was particularly useful in deterring eager fans desperate for a glimpse of their favourite author and possibly 'an autograph if Miss Dowson would oblige.' Miss Dowson made it a point of never obliging. She did not see it as her job to deal with fans turning up at her flat asking for her to sign copies of her books. Once the manuscript had left her possession, it was the publisher's responsibility to promote the novel and deal with over-enthusiastic readers.

Daisy entered her room some moments later. 'It's that Jacob Brown fellow. He says it's imperative he sees you on a private matter. He was most insistent. I thought it best to let him in. He's waiting for you in the sitting room.'

While Vivien Dowson was mildly irritated at being interrupted, she was also curious about this sudden visit of Jacob Brown, a man she hardly knew apart from the Murder Club meetings. She regarded him as a blustery uncouth individual who was very rough around his rural edges. What does the old devil want with me, she thought. 'Okay, Daisy. If it's a private matter, you'd better make yourself scarce.'

'Should I brew a pot of tea, Vivien?'

'No. I don't want to prolong the interview.' The thought of Brown lounging back in one of her armchairs, swilling down cups of tea and lighting numerous cigarettes, thus prolonging his stay, sent a shiver down her spine.

Dowson found Jacob Brown pacing up and down in an agitated fashion. His face was red and sweaty, and his tie askew.

'This is an unexpected pleasure,' she said smoothly in a fashion that made the sentiment sound almost genuine.

'Oh, Vivien, I'm in the most terrible fix. I need your help desperately,' he said with some anguish, mopping his brow with a spotted handkerchief. 'You're the only one I could think of who could help me.'

Daisy, who had secreted herself in the kitchen, out of the way, could not contain her curiosity and stood close to the door in an effort to listen in on the conversation taking place in the other room. The voices were muffled but soon became raised, and she was able to catch the odd phrase, one of which, uttered by the man, caused her to utter a gasp of surprise: 'You will have to bloody well help me,' Jacob Brown barked. 'Or else!'

It took a few seconds for Wilde to assimilate the startling news that Wilfred Collins had left, or 'escaped,' from Brandwell. It was clear from Dr Mellor's stoical expression that the latter was the case. 'That was rather careless of you, letting the blighter go,' he said bitterly. 'How on earth did that happen?'

Dr Mellor seemed unperturbed by the sarcastic brusqueness of her visitor's tone. 'This isn't a prison, Mr Wilde. We are not dealing with criminals, you know, just rather sad individuals with mental problems. Of course, certain inmates are locked in their rooms but that is for their own protection as well as that of others; however, some are given greater freedom—like Wilfred Collins. He had been here for several years and was suffering from a severe case of shell shock and had difficulty coping with the demands of reality, but he was in no way violent or a danger to himself, the staff, or other patients. As a result, about a year ago, he was allowed the privilege of trustee status. He obviously felt safe in this restricted environment, and gradually it seemed that a fragile normality was establishing itself in his behaviour. Wilfred felt secure here and no longer threatened by whatever dark forces his mind was prompted to invent. He worked a little in the kitchen and in the grounds, under supervision, of course. He was a placid, one might almost say a timid fellow.'

'And yet he escaped.'

'It is such an emotive word, don't you think? 'Escaped.' In reality, I believe he came to the conclusion that it was time for him to leave us.'

'How did he 'leave' you?'

'We believe he managed to stow away in the laundry van.'

'What action has been taken to try and trace him, bring him back?'

'Well, as I intimated earlier, he is not a criminal and as far as his assessments indicate he is no threat to anyone. Of course, the police were informed but for them he was just another missing person—there are so many of them now after the war. After all, he is not a miscreant on the run.'

'And this was three months ago.'

Dr Mellor gave a barely perceptive nod.

'And you have no idea where he is now.'

'I am afraid not. The police made enquiries but as there were no legal restraints on his freedom—as I already intimated, he isn't a criminal, just an invalid....'

'But an unstable one.'

Dr Mellor pursed her lips. 'He was vague and unworldly. He had reached a stage in his condition where any traces of innate anger within him had dissipated. He wouldn't and indeed couldn't harm a fly.'

'Are you sure?'

'Yes. In his time with us, he demonstrated no behaviour that suggested aggression or violence. In fact, quite the reverse. He was fearful of the unfamiliar. We felt that once he had tasted the real world again beyond the confines of the Brandwell walls, he would return to us.'

'But he hasn't.'

'Not as yet.'

'You still hold that belief?'

'Of course.'

In the metaphorical sense, Wilde bit his tongue. Either Dr Mellor was naive in the extreme, or she was attempting to make light of what was a major security failing. Even if Wilfred was merely an innocent abroad, with only his own safety at risk, the staff at Brandwell had proved incompetent in the extreme in dealing with him and, indeed, Dr Mellor's attitude demonstrated a strange lack of concern. It was obvious to Wilde that she was deliberately making light of the matter. Covering her own back was the phrase that sprang to his mind.

'What details do you have of his family?'

Dr Mellor consulted the file. 'Ah, yes. As far as we were able to ascertain, he was an orphan, both his parents having died in a motor accident some years before the war. He had a brother, but the authorities were unable to contact him.'

'And a sister?'

'Oh, yes.' Dr Mellor consulted her notes. 'Susan. Strange creature.'

'Why do you say that? Did you meet her?'

'On a few occasions. She visited her brother once or twice.'

'In what way was she strange?'

Dr Mellor pursed her lips. 'Difficult to say. It was more to do with my instinctive impression as a psychiatrist rather than any factual evidence. I sensed the same nervous instability in her manner as that exhibited by her brother. She tried to cover it with a kind of ebullient bravado, but it didn't fool me. No doubt the mental weakness was a family trait. She was a tall, thin, striking individual, with long dark hair and an extremely pale face.' We did not have much interaction—she was a woman of few words—few words with me, that is. However, Susan Collins was very affectionate and voluble when she was with her brother.'

'How did Wilfred react to these visits?'

'Very well, in one sense.'

'What do you mean, 'in one sense'?'

Dr Mellor adjusted his glasses and paused before replying. 'Well, he was always delighted to see 'his Bolly....'

"His Bolly'?'

'That's what he called her. I gather it was a childhood nickname that stuck. Apparently, her favourite champagne was Bollinger. As I say, he was always happy with her visits, but he became disturbed and uncooperative for a few

140

days afterwards. Her presence disturbed him. Most likely, the visits brought back fond memories of his childhood, a happy time, and when she left, it allowed the shadows to return.'

'I presume the police checked that Wilfred hadn't made a beeline for her place when he escaped.'

Dr Mellor nodded. 'I believe they could find no trace of her. The address she had given us was a false one.'

What is it with this family? mused Wilde darkly. They have a penchant for disappearing without a trace.

Her apparent lack of concern over this matter infuriated Wilde, but he kept his feelings in check. He certainly had learned very little from his visit to Brandwell that would be of use to him. He could not relieve himself of the impression that Dr Mellor was being particularly unhelpful in the matter, as though she was keeping some information back, something that would place her in a bad light.

She rose from her chair, a definite gesture to indicate that the interview was over, but Wilde wasn't quite finished yet.

'You say that you think that Wilfred will return to you one day.'

Dr Mellor nodded.

'So, you have kept his room in readiness for such an eventuality.'

Dr Mellor's eyes widened. She could see where this was going, but she responded without having the time to censor herself. 'Yes.' The word slipped out unbidden, and she cursed herself silently for being so careless.

Wilde smiled and nodded. 'I'd like to see his room, please?'

'I'm afraid....'

'Surely rather me than the police. I am investigating a murder...'

Dr Mellor held still for a moment, indecision marking her features. 'Very well,' she said at length with a sigh.

The room was little more than a cell: featureless white walls, a bed, a chair, a sink, and a desk. Wilde thought that the sense of despair and confinement which hung like an invisible mist in the room was enough to unhinge even the sanest of men.

Dr Mellor stood sentinel at the door while Wilde walked around the room, scrutinising everything, looking for something, anything that would help him with this mystery. It seemed there was nothing, until he came to the desk. There was a vase of dead flowers perched on the top, the stems dropping over the edge as though mourning their own demise. A little card lay nearby with the inscription 'Love from B. Murder at Midnight.'

Well, thought Wilde, the B obviously stood for Bolly, the nickname of his sister, but what on earth did Murder at Midnight mean? He stored the phrase away to ponder on later.

There were a few blank sheets of paper. A pen and a bottle of ink, along with a book. It was a crime novel entitled *Death Comes to The Party*. Wilde felt a tingle at the back of his neck when he saw that the author was Ambrose De Lacy. On the blank flyleaf, there was a minute drawing of a dagger with spots representing blood dripping from its blade. Wilde then turned his attention to the title page. He was chilled to see that the author's name had been obliterated by black ink with vicious strokes of the pen.

'Are we done?' The brittle tone of Dr Mellor's voice broke into his thoughts.

'Almost,' said Wilde. There is just one more question I'd like to ask you about Susan Collins....'

On his journey back to London, he thought hard about what he had seen and heard and that cryptic phrase 'Murder at Midnight.' He wondered, perhaps, whether it was another thriller by Ambrose De Lacy. It was something that he'd better find out. If it was, maybe the plot would give him some much-desired clues. And then, more importantly, there was that little detail that Dr Mellor had revealed about Wilfred's sister.

On reaching the city, Wilde made his way to Hatchard's bookshop. 'Could you tell me if there's an Ambrose De Lacy called *Murder at Midnight*?' he asked the white-haired assistant who peered at him through a pair of golden pince-nez.

'Oh, no, sir, definitely not. We have all Mr De Lacy's volumes in stock, and that title is not one of them.'

'Ah, well, thank you,' muttered Wilde with some disappointment, but just as he was about to turn away, the salesman continued.

'However, we do have a copy of *Murder at Midnight* by Meg Granger, one of the newer lady crime writers. And very good it is.'

'Do you, by Jove? Meg Granger, eh? Well, I'd like a copy of that….'

'It shall be yours, sir. If you'll wait a moment, I will retrieve one for you.'

After obtaining his copy of *Murder at Midnight*, Wilde repaired to a nearby coffee shop and investigated his new purchase. Disappointingly, the author details on the flyleaf were sketchy, giving no real biography of Miss Granger apart from the fact that she wrote most of the novel when she was recovering from a long illness. It did not state what that was. The book must have been popular and successful, for this was its third impression. That was no doubt why she had been scooped up by De Lacy for the Murder Club. He quickly skimmed the first chapter and found it pleasantly engaging but little more. He began constructing a little scenario in his mind based on the evidence he had collected, which would explain why this title had been written down by Wilfred Collins' sister. He cast his mind back to the meeting of the Murder Club and his encounter with Meg Granger. It was an encounter that now tantalised him, particularly after the answer Dr Mellor had given him to his final question.

Chapter Twenty-Eight

That evening Wilde dined with Kishen in a little restaurant new to them in Soho. 'Best not to frequent our usual haunts at present. You never know if our murderous friend will still be watching,' Wilde had observed.

'Do you think that is possible?'

'It is possible, but not likely, to be honest. They saw the blaze in the old building, and no doubt they have read the obituary. I think the devil will be satisfied, but it's always best to be cautious, old lad, when the situation allows.'

During dinner, Wilde recounted his experience at Brandwell. 'And so, we have another loose end with the sister. Both she and bother Daniel have shrunk into the shadows hiding away from the light, along with Wilfred. If only we knew where they were.'

'Or at least one of them.'

Wilde nodded and smiled. 'Yes, one would do for a start.'

'And this Dr Mellor was of no real help to you.'

'Not really. She was certainly not about to let any cats out of her particular bag, and I'm sure there were a few. She was determined to make light of Wilfred's escape and the fact that he was of no threat to the outside world.'

'Do you believe her?'

Wilde thought for a moment. 'Not really. However, the lady isn't a criminal; she is just protecting herself and, to a lesser degree Brandwell itself. I've been in touch with Johnny Ferguson to see if he can find out if Wilfred Collins' escape was actually reported to the police.'

Kishen's eyes widened in shock.

'You think she may have lied about that.'

Wilde dabbed his chin with a napkin. 'I wouldn't put it past her.'

'That is terrible.'

'If it's true. I may be being overly suspicious, but it's a trait that comes with the territory.'

'So, you learned nothing of importance from your visit.'

'Not quite.' Wilde told Kishen about the sketches on the notepaper and De Lacy's novel. But he did keep one detail to himself. He was savouring it, playing with it, attempting to slot it into the growing scenario of the mystery which was forming in his mind.

'What do you make of all that?' asked Kishen.

'The drawings were quite childlike, but there was a vicious quality about them. It is difficult to explain. I suppose it's more an impression I gained rather than actual fact, but the black ink, which I saw as representing blood, was strangely upsetting and ominous. It implied a kind of suppressed anger and incipient violence in the artist.'

'What does it all mean?'

Wilde gave a weary shake of the head. 'I am not absolutely certain, but one thing is clear, it is imperative that we find Wilfred Collins and soon.'

'And the murderer is....' The typewriter keys stopped clacking as Vivien Dowson reached this critical point in her manuscript. Now she had to take the decision that would make the whole novel work, surprising the reader and garnering splendid reviews. When she started writing a new mystery, she planned it with meticulous care, always knowing who the guilty party was, but in the final stages of composition, she invariably changed her mind regarding the murderer, based on the notion that if she knew the identity of the miscreant from the beginning, so would the reader. In this instance, it was supposed to be the Reverend Sheldon, the cleric with the gammy leg, but he had behaved so suspiciously throughout the story that he really had become too obvious. This was the way with some characters: they took on a life of their own and overplayed their role. And so now Vivien had to decide who would take his place and end up on the gallows. There were really only two prime contenders, Sheldon's wife, the rather narcissistic manic flower arranger, or Thornton, the schoolteacher with the eyepatch.

As she deliberated over the choice, the doorbell rang. She glanced up at the clock on the mantelpiece. It was nearing midnight. Who on earth would be calling at this time of night? A chill thought struck her. It could be that obnoxious Jacob Brown here to solicitate her help again in his disgusting, illegal scheme. She imagined him having retired with his tail between his legs after his previous visit, and then fuelled himself with alcohol in readiness for a second attempt. As these thoughts passed through her mind, the doorbell rang again with a forceful, insistent chime.

With some trepidation, Vivien Dowson made her way from the study, and as she passed through the sitting room, she retrieved a poker from the hearth. Taking a deep breath, she approached her front door.

'Who is it?' she called out in stentorian tones.

For a moment, there was silence, and then the doorbell rang again, followed by a fist beating on the door.

'The fool,' muttered Vivien, her dander rising. 'He'll wake the whole building'. Reluctantly, she unchained the door and withdrew the catch. Grasping the poker firmly in her hand, she opened the door. Standing before her was a shadowy figure, their features hidden in the gloom.

'Hello, Vivien,' a voice intoned in such a way that Vivien froze with fear, the poker sliding from her hand, landing with a gentle thump on the carpet.

Chapter Twenty-Nine

The day following his visit to Brandwell, Wilde busied himself trying to find out more about Wilfred Collins. With Kishen in tow, he made an early visit to the War Office, which had allowed him to discover an address where Wilfred had lived before he joined the army. Unfortunately, it was a rented apartment, and the current owner had never met him. It seemed that everywhere he turned in this investigation, he was met by a brick wall. Somewhat disillusioned with things, he tried to cheer himself up by popping into a telephone box and putting a call through to Sally in Brighton but met another brick wall. Her aunt told him she was out shopping.

'Not my day, Kishen, my friend. However, let's try one more avenue before lunch.'

'And which avenue is that?'

'Blackstone's the publishers. They have offices in the Strand.'

It was at Blackstone's that Wilde passed himself off as a feature writer for the prestigious literary magazine *Book World*. 'We are preparing a series about new up-and-coming mystery writers and our first piece will be on Meg Granger, and I'd like to get a little background as to how her first book was published.' he explained to the pert receptionist. His performance was sufficiently convincing that he and Kishen ('my secretary') were taken down a labyrinth of corridors to meet the head of the modern fiction department, Arnold Strong, a man not much older than Wilde. He was a tall untidy individual with a mop of unruly blonde hair. He wore a fair isle jumper over a white open-necked shirt and a pair of baggy tweed trousers. His office was a little like the man himself: untidy and shabby, but Wilde could see from his keen blue eyes that there was a bright intelligence there.

'Ah, so you want to know about the mysterious Meg, eh? Well, good luck to you, gentlemen.'

'Why mysterious?'

'I know little about her apart from the fact that she's a pretty good mystery writer, as indicated by *Murder at Midnight*. We're still waiting for her next. She's a little overdue with that one. But that is often the case with second novels.' He pulled a thin file from the top drawer of his desk. 'This is all I have on her, and it's mainly press reviews. No background stuff at all.'

'Could you let me have her address?'

Strong shook his head. 'Sorry. I'd need to contact her to see if she is agreeable to me passing on such information. And I can tell you now, she won't be. Miss Granger is a very private person.'

'How did she get to be published by you?' Wilde asked, taking out his cigarette case and lighting one.

'Her manuscript just landed on my desk,' Strong replied casually. 'We get a lot of unsolicited scripts arriving daily. Unlike some publishers, we don't dismiss them out of hand. We have a small team of readers who skim the first fifty pages or so. If any show some promise, they are passed on to me or one of the other senior editors. I was just lucky enough to be handed Meg's little gem. I could see we had a winner on our hands with that one.'

'I gather she wrote a great deal of the novel while she was convalescing.'

'Yes, so she informed us.'

'What had she been suffering from?'

Strong gave a little chuckle. 'Ah, that also remains a mystery. She told me in no uncertain terms that this was a personal matter and had nothing to do with her writing career. She was simply telling me to mind my own business. I am usually very good at wheedling information from my writers, but I failed in this instance. I must admit, in our few meetings, she always seemed physically healthy, but her personality was, how shall I put it, prone to drama. One could never be sure what kind of mood she was in when she came in the office to discuss her work. But then all writers are a bit that way, y'know. It comes from possessing a vivid imagination and from having to be judged by editors, by the critics, and the public.'

'And so you know nothing of her background or family,' said Wilde extracting his cigarette case. He offered it to Strong, who shook his head.

'Do you mind if I do?'

'Sure. Go ahead.'

'Well,' said Wilde after lighting up, '...as I was saying: family background. Is there anything at all that you can tell me?'

Strong shook his head. 'Nothing concrete. She was well educated and obviously from reasonably comfortable circumstances. She had expensive tastes and was always smartly dressed. However, I know nothing of her parents or siblings—if there were any.'

'Romance? Men friends?'

'Nothing there either. Sorry I can't be of any more help. Your headline is obviously going to be 'Mystery writer is a Mystery.'

Wilde gave an exaggerated sigh. 'Well, thank you for your time.' Wilde rose and then looked a little confused. 'How does one get out of this building?' he asked, grinning.

Strong returned the grin. 'Yes, it is a bit of a warren, isn't it. Let me show you the way.' He leapt from his seat and led them into the corridor. 'This way, gentlemen,' he cried as though he was leading a party of explorers into the unknown. They hadn't got very far before Wilde gave an exclamation of surprise which halted their progress. 'I'm awfully sorry, but I'm afraid I left my cigarette case in your office. Bear with me while I pop back to get it.'

As he hared off back down the corridor, Kishen grinned. 'I hope he doesn't get lost,' he said.

A few minutes later, Wilde returned. 'Sorry about that,' he said lightly, holding up his cigarette case.

'What was all that cigarette case business about? You left it behind on purpose, didn't you?' he said once they were making their way back to the car.

'Of course, I did. It was a way to extract a little bit of information. There is more than one way to skin a cat, y'know.'

'Ugh. An old English adage which is quite repulsive. What information did you 'extract?''

'I dipped into that file Strong so carelessly left on his desk, and I managed to get Miss Granger's address.'

'What makes you so interested in this Granger lady?'

Wilde told him about the title of her book being written on a card in Wilfred Collins' room at Brandwell. 'And there is one other piece of evidence that clinches the connection between Collins and Miss Granger.'

'Oh, what is that?'

Wilde told him.

'Good gracious,' Kishen said wide-eyed, making no attempt to disguise the surprise in his voice.

Wilde sighed. 'Good gracious, indeed. Now let's high-tail it back home. I am in desperate need of a large gin and tonic'.

Just as they entered the flat, the telephone began to ring. Slipping off his overcoat and flinging it on the chair, Wilde snatched up the receiver, hoping it might be Sally. He waited to hear the caller's voice. It was Johnny Ferguson.

'Your little drama has just turned a shade darker, my friend. There's been another murder?'

'Who?'

'A second member of that Murder Club of yours. Vivien Dowson.'

Wilde felt a heavy weight fall upon his body. He did not know what to say at first. The implications of such a crime caused his mind to spin into free fall. 'Give me the details?' he finally managed to croak from a dry throat.

'Her daily woman found her this morning. She had been savagely beaten about the head—rather in the same way that Carfax was. Same modus operandi as we Scotland Yard types say.'

'Is it in the press yet?'

'No, but it will be in the morning.'

For an instant, Wilde had an image of Ambrose De Lacy reading the early edition and his hysterical reaction to the revelation.

'Because of you, Rupert, and the Carfax killing, I've poked my nose into the investigation of Dowson's murder. It was Inspector Jackson's brief, but I muscled in and pulled rank. I thought it might be useful if we worked in tandem on the case.'

The ghost of a smile manifested itself on Wilde's lips. 'You old dog. Of course, it would,' he said, his spirits already lightening. 'I need to see the scene of the crime and have a chat with Dowson's maid.'

'Of course. All can be arranged. If you've got something to write with, I can give you Dowson's address and will meet you there in half an hour.'

'Brilliant.' Wilde snatched up a pencil and pad he kept by the telephone. 'Go ahead.'

Detective Inspector Johnny Ferguson was waiting for them when Wilde and Kishen arrived at Vivien Dowson's flat. It was clear where the murder had taken place; a large dark red blood stain in the hallway bore witness to the violence.

'I reckon the old girl didn't stand a chance. Head bashed in with some force. The police surgeon reckoned it only took two blows to kill her,' said Ferguson lighting up a cigarette before offering his packet to Wilde and Kishen. Both men refused.

'Mind if we scout around?' asked Wilde.

'Be my guest. Our boys have already given the place a thorough search, but they didn't exactly know what they were looking for. You may know better.'

Wilde gave a tight grin. 'I wouldn't bet on it. At the moment, I'm putting all my faith in luck. This case seemed such a simple affair, to begin with, but now I feel I'm swimming out of my depth.'

'I'll have a look in the bedroom,' said Kishen.

'Right you are. I'll tackle the lair where she conjured up her mysteries. Which one is that, Johnny?'

The inspector directed him.

It was a neat and tidy study with a large table bearing the weight of a huge typewriter. There were a few bookcases and a drinks trolley, a chaise longue, and a stiff bentwood chair by the desk. Just uncomfortable enough to keep the lady author writing and not relaxing. There was a sheet of paper in the typewriter. Wilde examined it. There were just three words on the page: 'The murderer is...' Wilde gave a dry bitter chuckle. 'That's what I'd like to know,' he murmured to himself.

He began searching the drawers, hoping he would find something to throw a light on the mystery, possibly a note similar to those received by De Lacy warning Vivien Dowson of her impending doom. But he found nothing apart from plot notes for a novel—no doubt the one she had been writing and in which had been about to reveal the name of the murderer

In scouring the rest of the room, his attention was caught by a small, framed photograph on the mantelpiece. It was of a whitewashed cottage nestling in a large garden. In the background he observed the sea. As he gazed at it, an electric charge ran through his body. 'By George!' he exclaimed, picking up the photograph frame and examining the picture more closely. He had seen that cottage before or rather a sketch of it—in Ambrose De Lacy's flat. What added to his interest was the name of the cottage printed in capitals at the bottom of the photograph: 'ROSEMULLION'.

Daisy Blackburn, Dowson's cleaner, lived only a few streets away in a small, terraced house. On opening the door, she peered out suspiciously and then recognised Ferguson whom she had met earlier in the day.

'You again,' she said not unpleasantly.

'Sorry to bother you, Mrs Blackburn—'

'Miss, if you don't mind,' she interrupted with a derogatory sniff.

'Oh, I'm sorry.'

'Why is it that folk always assume that when you reach my time of life, you must be married? I have or never have had any inclination to be shackled to a man.'

Ferguson nodded. 'Quite. I apologise for being presumptuous.'

'I should think so.'

'Actually, we'd like to come in and ask you a few more questions. It would be a great help if you could assist in this way, Miss Blackburn.'

'But I've told you all what I know.'

'There are certain things that have cropped up that only you can help us with. You are a very important person in this enquiry.'

'Really? Is that so? Very important, eh?' she said, her eyes brightening and her somewhat flinty demeanour melting a little.

'Indubitably.'

'And who are your cronies?' She looked past Ferguson and cast a suspicious eye on Wilde and Kishen.

'They are colleagues working with me on the investigation. May we come in?'

Miss Blackburn hesitated for a moment and then held the door open and, with a vague gesture, bid them enter. She led them into a neat but cramped sitting room. A cat lay curled up on the rug before a coal fire. 'Sit yourself down,' she said, indicating a small sofa as she slumped into an easy chair opposite.

Ferguson and Wilde perched awkwardly on the edge of the sofa. Kishen stood quietly by the door.

'So, what do you want to know?' asked Miss Blackburn, taking up her knitting, which had been abandoned on a small table at the side of her chair.

'I know you've been asked this before, but have you any idea who might have committed the dreadful crime?'

Miss Blackburn shook her head. 'No. Vivien—I always called her Vivien, there was no false formality between us—led a fairly quiet life. I suppose you could say she put all her excitement into her books.' She chuckled. 'Well, I assume that. To be honest, I never read any one of them.'

'She never mentioned someone to you whom she felt nervous about?' probed Ferguson.

'No.' And then she paused dramatically as though a thought had struck her. 'Oh, there was that other writer chap who came and was pretty obnoxious.'

'Which writer?'

She thought for a moment. 'Er... Brown. Yes, that's it, Brown, Jacob Brown.'

'In what way was he obnoxious?' asked Wilde. It was the first time he had spoken, and Miss Blackburn glanced at him suspiciously. She was naturally apprehensive when dealing with posh chaps.

'Well,' she said after a brief pause, 'he came the other day to see Vivien on what he called 'private business', so I was ushered into the kitchen while the two of them had a chinwag.'

'You had no idea what this private business was all about?'

'Not really, but this Brown fellow got well and truly aerated, I can tell you that. I could hear his angry voice booming. I do remember hearing him say something like 'you'll have to help me or else!' As I say, he was obnoxious about it. 'Or else,' he said. It was certainly some sort of threat.'

'And you have no idea what he meant by that?'

'No idea whatsoever, and Vivien didn't mention it to me. I think she just dismissed the incident from her mind. It didn't seem to upset her in the slightest.'

Ferguson and Wilde exchanged frustrated glances.

'Look, I think I've told you all I know. You don't want me to make things up, do you?'

'Certainly not,' said Ferguson with a smile. 'Well, thank you for your time.'

Both men rose to leave, but as they reached the door, Wilde turned back towards Miss Blackburn. 'Do you know anything about a little whitewashed cottage and the name Rosemullion?'

The woman grinned. 'Of course, I do. It's Vivien's cottage on the coast, on the cliffs near Falmouth. An area called Coral Point. It's her retreat. She goes there to write when a book is proving to be difficult.'

'Does she always go alone?'

'Oh, yes. She can't write with other people around. But she did let one or two other people use it when she wasn't there.'

'Anyone in particular?'

'There was a niece of hers, Jean, and that other writer…what's his name? A posh one.'

'Ambrose De Lacy,' prompted Wilde.

Miss Blackburn nodded her head decisively. 'That's the fellow. Rather a pompous individual who fancies himself a bit if you ask me, but Vivien seemed to like him.'

'So he went down to the cottage?'

'Yes, I believe so - on a few occasions.'

'On his own?'

'Oh, I couldn't say. You'll have to ask Vivien…oh, of course, you can't. Oh, dear.' Suddenly Miss Blackburn's eyes moistened, and her voice faltered. 'Here I am talking about her as though she was still alive…and she isn't, she's…' She scrabbled in the pocket of her dress for a handkerchief and dabbed her eyes. 'I don't know what I'm going to do now she's gone.'

The three men repaired to a local hostelry for refreshment and to confer over what they had learned about the case that evening. 'Well, it seems to me we have two distinct leads now,' Wilde. 'There's the cottage in Cornwall, Rosemullion, and the threats made by Dowson's fellow Murder Club member, Jacob Brown.'

'What do you know of him?' asked Ferguson, nursing his whisky glass in both hands.

'Not much. I've only met the chap the once. He didn't strike me as the violent type, but then these fellows have ways of hiding such things.'

'I thought there was a streak of arrogance, which was not at all pleasant,' observed Kishen.

Ferguson nodded. 'I'll certainly need to have a word with him. Dig a little deeper. But what about this cottage? Why do you think that is so important, Rupert?'

Wilde told Ferguson of finding the note bearing the word 'Rosemullion' in De Lacy's wastepaper basket. 'It was on the same notepaper in the same hand and purple ink as the threatening letter De Lacy received. However, he didn't want me to see it. I'm not sure why, but it does suggest he is trying to hide something from me, something which may have dark repercussions for him. Why should someone send him a note like that? It was in some way a threat, a warning, and now we find out that De Lacy actually visited the cottage bearing that name. That is something Kishen and I must follow up, but first, I reckon we should check on Mr Jacob Brown'.

Chapter Thirty

Unaware that he was about to receive three visitors who would throw a dark shadow across his life, Jacob Brown was feeding the hens on his smallholding near Stroud in the Cotswolds. It was a fine brisk spring morning and Brown, a true country man in spirit, dallied over his task, enjoying the shafts of pale yellow sunshine and the cool breeze on his cheek. This is where his heart was: in green rolling pastures and fresh, unsullied air, not in the smoky concrete warren of London. Not for the first time, he contemplated giving up this writing lark and just settling for the simple rural life. He reckoned he had made enough money from his writing to allow this to happen. There was just one cloud on the horizon—but it was a bloody big cloud, he reckoned. He shuddered with emotion when he recalled what he had done when that annoying cow Vivien had refused to help him. What he had been forced to do. Curse her. She had left him with no alternative. Well, to his way of thinking, he had no real alternative. Through writing about crime, and murders in particular, he was well aware of the risks involved in his actions. He just wanted to blank it from his mind and hope to God there would be no repercussions.

As he was mooching over these thoughts, a motorcar trundled down the narrow lane and pulled up outside his house. Three men got out, and from their stern expressions, it was clear they were not particularly happy. As they approached him Brown recognised two of them. There was that private detective chap who had given some spiel the other night at the club and his Indian mate. What the hell were they doing here?

'Mr Brown. We'd like to have a few words with you,' said the tall, dark-haired man he didn't recognise.

'What about?'' came Brown's brusque response as he found his chest tightening with apprehension.

'I am Detective Inspector John Ferguson of Scotland Yard, and I believe you know these other gentlemen.'

'Scotland Yard? Police? What the devil do you want with me?' A fine sheen of sweat began to materialise on his forehead. He did not like this one bit.

'Can we go inside? It will be more conducive for our…chat.'

Simple though it was, there was something ominous about this request, and Brown felt his body grow tense.

'I suppose so,' he agreed reluctantly and led the three men to the house and into the kitchen. It was a small, desperately untidy room. The sink was full of unwashed crockery. The shabby dresser had a fine covering of dust, and the table was littered with papers and books in an *ad hoc* fashion. A rickety chest in the alcove had various items of clothing peeping out from unclosed drawers.

'I apologise for the…er mess, gentlemen,' he said casually. 'My cleaning girl has suddenly gone absent without leave. Not much of a tidy soul myself, I'm afraid, but then I've only got myself to look after. Anyway, down to business, gentlemen: what brings Scotland Yard out to the sticks on this bright Spring morning? Not selling tickets to the policeman's ball, I'll be bound.' Brown's attempt at humour was awkward and forced. Wilde noticed that he was clenching and unclenching his fists in a nervous manner.

'Something a little more serious, sir,' said Ferguson evenly. 'You will have heard about the death of Vivien Dowson….'

Brown's mouth gaped, and his frame stiffened with shock. A mixture of emotions fizzed in his brain. So they weren't here about Sadie, he thought, with some relief. He felt the tightness in his chest ease—but what the hell had happened to the Dowson woman? 'Vivien… dead?' he managed to croak at length. 'No, I've heard nothing about that. How the hell did it happen?' He was about to add that she had seemed in the prime of health the last time he'd seen her but swiftly had second thoughts about that, remembering the circumstances of their recent encounter.

'I am sorry to say that Miss Dowson was murdered. Killed in her own flat.'

'Lord o' mercy! That is terrible.'

'Indeed.'

'But what's that got to do with me?'

'We believe you visited her recently and were involved in an altercation. To put it bluntly, Mr Brown, you threatened her.'

The author shook his head vigorously. 'I did no such thing.'

'Be careful what you say, Mr Brown,' warned Ferguson. 'We have a witness who states you said, 'You'll have to help me or else.' That, in my book, is a threat.'

'Nonsense. There was no one present during our meeting.'

'Miss Blackburn, Miss Dowson's cleaning lady, was in the kitchen and overheard you.'

'Overheard—'

'She heard you use those words to Miss Dowson. What help were you trying to get from her?'

You're a writer, his mind screamed. You make things up for a living. So bloody well make things up now!

The three men watched as the blood drained from Brown's features, and his eyes flickering wildly as he tried to manufacture a good lie to satisfy them.

'Did you murder Miss Dowson?' It was Wilde who proffered this question. He could see that Brown was in some sort of mental quandary and knew that such a question would unnerve him further. It was a calculated attempt to get at the truth.

But the veiled accusation seemed to rally Brown. He shook his head vigorously. 'No, no, did I hell. That's bloody ridiculous. I…I may have said those words because I was angry. We all say dramatic stuff when we are roused.'

'So, I repeat, what help had you asked for that Miss Dowson refused to give you?' asked Ferguson.

Brown knew he couldn't tell them the truth. That would certainly help to put a rope around his neck. He gave a sweaty rictus smile to indicate what he was about to reveal had no real dark implications. 'I…er…simply needed some cash. I'd lost a bit at the races, and I just wanted a couple of hundred to tide me over till my royalty cheque arrived. I was really down in the dumps about it and had a few more drinks than I should. It was a foolish thing to do, calling on Vivien for a loan. I know that, and I admit I behaved badly, but I did not touch a hair of her head. Why would I? What would I gain?'

'Did you manage to obtain the two hundred pounds from somewhere?' asked Kishen gently.

Brown gave him a fierce glance. 'What the hell has that got to do with you…?'

'Kishen is part of my detective team,' said Ferguson.

'He's just Wilde's punkawallah.'

'Insults are not called for, Mr Brown. Kishen is helping me with my enquiries and I'd be obliged if you would treat him with respect and answer his question: did you manage to get your two hundred pounds from somewhere else?'

Another pause from Brown before his stilted reply. 'I hocked a few of my precious first editions if you must know.'

Ferguson did not believe him, but he changed the direction of his questioning. 'Have you any idea who might want to kill Vivien Dowson?'

'No idea whatsoever. She was a harmless soul. As far as I can tell, she led a quiet and simple life. All the drama was in her stories. I am truly sorry to hear about her death. Can't say any more.'

Ferguson gave a sigh and pursed his lips. 'Well, thank you for your time, Mr Brown. We may need to interview you again and obtain a statement from you, but for the moment, we'll leave you in peace,' he said and began moving towards the door, followed by Wilde and Kishen.

The stranger treated themselves to a pleasant lunch with wine in a smart restaurant in Chelsea. It was the prize for getting so far with their plans. 'We're on the last stretch now,' they murmured, lifting the cool glass of Sancerre in a self-satisfied toast.

Chapter Thirty-One

Sally sat in a seafront café in Brighton. She had been absent-mindedly stirring her tea for about a minute while her mind was elsewhere. She gazed out of the café windows, gently misted by a recent light shower, not really focusing on the promenade that was visible across the road. She was trying to come to terms with the conflicting thoughts that were dancing around in her brain. She was unsure whether to dismiss them or accept them as sensible and practical. A decision had to be made and it must be made soon, otherwise, it would be unfair. Whichever path she took, she must be certain and resolute.

For a moment her reverie was interrupted by the noisy entrance into the café of a young couple, giggling and exchanging affectionate glances. Within moments they had settled at a table and were holding hands. Sally turned away and gazed down at her arm and saw the ugly bruise there. Viewing it made her flinch. That dark blemish and the tenderness it generated seemed a pivotal issue in the tussle of thoughts in her tired mind. Deep down, she knew what the sensible course of action was, but her emotions were at odds with this. She sighed heavily and withdrew the spoon from her tea, laid it down gently in the saucer, and stared unseeingly at the pale brown liquid as it swirled gently in the cup.

'Well,' said Ferguson as he drove away from Jacob Brown's smallholding, 'there's something going on there. The man was as nervous as a kitten.'

'I agree,' said Wilde,' but I don't think it had anything to do Vivien Dowson's murder. There was something else that was making him edgy. He almost seemed relieved when you explained the reason for our visit, as though he had been expecting it to be about another matter altogether.'

'Indeed,' said Kishen, 'this punkawallah received the same impression.'

'The arrogant bastard to call you that,' said Ferguson.

Kishen gave a gentle shrug of the shoulder. 'I've been called worse.'

'I can think of a fine phrase to call the bounder,' said Wilde. 'It's certainly clear, Johnny, old boy, that you'll need to keep an eye on Mr Jacob Brown.'

The policeman gave a knowing smile. 'Have no fear. That point has already been noted.'

As they were passing through the village, Wilde leaned forward and peered through the car windscreen. 'I say, there's a neat little pub up ahead. How about grabbing a spot of lunch before the drive back to London?'

The Ash Tree was a typical, simple but warm and inviting country inn. There was a fire blazing in the grate and the walls were adorned with various ancient farming implements. There were a few local drinkers leaning at the bar and a chubby red-faced landlord behind the counter who gave his new customers a warm greeting. 'Food is it, gentleman?' he said cheerily in response to their enquiry. 'Well, our fare is simple but good. How about a ploughman's lunch, cheese, pork pie, and a few hot new potatoes?' Wilde and his companions nodded in agreement. This was supplemented with two pints of ale and a ginger beer for Kishen.

Wilde picked up a leaflet from the bar as they moved to one of the dining tables near the fire.

'What have you got there?' asked Ferguson after taking a drink of beer.

'A village girl has gone missing. It's asking if anyone has seen her. There's her picture,' he said, passing the leaflet to Ferguson. 'Pretty little thing. Looks like a teenager.'

The policeman perused the leaflet with interest. 'Name of Sadie Thompson. Worked as a cleaner in several houses in the village. Been missing for just a few days. Another of life's little tragedies.'

Kishen picked up the leaflet, and his eyes widened with interest. 'I say, look at the cardigan the girl is wearing. That odd pink and blue striped design.'

"What about it?' asked Ferguson.

Kishen shut his eyes for a moment as though he was trying to remember something. 'I've seen that cardigan, that pattern before. Today,' he said slowly, still keeping his eyes closed. 'Yes, yes,' he added excitedly, his eyes flashing open brightly. You remember Mr Brown's untidy kitchen. That chest with items hanging out. It was there—that cardigan. A small section draping from one of the drawers.'

Kishen's two companions stared at him for a few moments without a word. It was Wilde who was the first one to speak. 'By George, I believe you are right. Well done, my friend. Brown did say that his cleaner had gone absent without leave—so why did he have her cardigan? Or, indeed, any female attire? That raises a very pertinent question. Something smells odd here.'

'Indeed, I believe we are on to something untoward,' agreed Ferguson. 'That would explain why the fellow was so twitchy. It was nothing to do with the death of Vivien Dowson...

'...but with the disappearance of Sadie Thompson, his cleaning lady,' said Kishen finishing the sentence.

The three men looked at each other with suppressed excitement in their glances.

'I think we need to have further words with Mr Jacob Brown,' said Rupert Wilde.

Fifteen minutes later, they were driving back to Brown's farm. During the journey, Wilde suggested their plan of action to which the others agreed. 'We have to be brutal and confident that we know everything, despite the fact that we don't,' he said.

Brown was about to settle down to a ham sandwich when there came a knock at the door. 'What now?' he muttered, pushing his plate aside. He was unnerved to find Wilde and his two companions on his doorstep once more.

'You again! Can't you leave a fellow in peace?' I've told you all I know.'

'We don't believe that to be true', said Wilde. 'We need to come in and question you further.'

'Bloody hell!' Brown appeared more angry than worried as he stood back to let the three men into his kitchen once more. Each of them cast a glance at the chest in the alcove and saw the section of cardigan still hanging from the partially open drawer.

'What d'you want to know this time?' growled Brown.

'Quite simply, we want to know where Sadie Thompson is. What have you done with her?'

Brown's eyes widened with fear, and he fell back a few steps. His mouth moved silently as though he was about to speak, but the words wouldn't come. And then, in an instant, he turned and ran. He raced to the back of the kitchen and into a passageway, and out through the back door. The three men followed, with Kishen leading the way.

Brown had traversed the lawn, leapt over the garden wall, and headed down the lane.

'The fool,' snapped Ferguson. 'He can't possibly get away.'

Indeed, Kishen was close on his heels, and just as Brown reached the end of the lane leading to the main road, Kishen launched himself at his quarry and, in a flying tackle, brought him to the ground. Within seconds Ferguson and Wilde were at his side, hauling Brown to his feet.

'Very nice tackle, Kishen. Quite professional.'

Kishen grinned. 'I played rugby at school—in the first eleven.'

They marched Brown to the house, where Ferguson clapped on a pair of handcuffs. 'I always carry a pair in case of emergencies,' he said with a dark grin.

Brown had remained silent since he had been apprehended and now sat on a kitchen stool, his head bowed.

'I think it would be best to tell us the story now,' said Wilde. 'You know you'll feel better if you get the whole thing off your chest, out of your mind.'

Brown gave a disparaging laugh. 'Out of my mind? I'll never get it out of my mind. I did wrong, and nothing can change that.'

'Tell us about it,' said Ferguson. 'The truth, mind you.'

Brown shook his head wearily. It was a gesture of sadness rather than denial.

'Sadie is dead, isn't she?' said Wilde.

Brown gazed at him, tears welling up. 'Yes,' he said softly, almost a whisper.

Ferguson picked up a bottle of whisky from the table, poured a large glassful, and handed it to Brown. 'Come on,' he said gently. 'Time to tell the truth.'

Brown took a large gulp from the glass, his body shivering slightly with the effects of the alcohol invading his body.

'I was very fond of Sadie,' he began. 'She was a simple lass, but sweet and obliging. She hadn't experienced much love in her short life. Violent father who left when she was ten and alcoholic mother who showed no interest in the girl. She came here to clean for me twice a week. We got on fine. Despite the difference in our ages, she felt comfortable with me. We...grew close. It was pleasing to me to have feminine company at my time of life. Well, things accelerated, as you might say. I treated her well, treated her kindly, and she responded. I suppose it started with a hug, a cuddle, and then...kissing. It made us both feel happy...wanted. And then we went further. She took to spending some nights with me here.

It was all very pleasant until... until she found out that she was pregnant.' Brown gave a bitter laugh. 'That really put the cat amongst the pigeons. I think we both knew she couldn't have the baby. I'm sure you can guess the reasons. Scandal and so on. I certainly didn't want to be tied down to a bastard child, and neither did she. Poor Sadie was not mentally equipped to cope with the demands of motherhood. So it had to be an abortion.'

'And that's where Vivien Dowson came into the picture,' said Wilde, already ahead of the game, piecing bits of the jigsaw together,

Brown nodded. 'Yes. She had been a nurse, and I was hoping that she would help me bring about a termination. But she wouldn't. She refused point blank—said the whole business was morally repugnant. I was at my wit's end. And then suddenly, Sadie changed her mind. She decided she wanted to keep the baby. The stupid girl. We rowed and fought about it. Things got out of hand...' Brown paused, tears streaking down his face, and with a jerky movement, downed the remainder of the whisky. 'Things got...really out of hand.'

'You killed her,' said Ferguson softly.

'Yes. May God forgive me. I didn't mean to. I just…I lost my mind, I guess. She kept screaming, 'It's my baby, my body. I want my baby.' What had got into her, I don't know. I couldn't reason with her. I couldn't shut her up. I grabbed her, put my hand over her mouth to stop her words, but she wouldn't stop. 'I want my baby,' she screamed. Before I knew what was happening, I had my hands around her throat. I was willing her to stop. Willing her to be silent….'

Brown put his head in his hands and began to sob, his body heaving with emotion. It was a wretched sight, and the three men stood in silent disgust and waited until Brown brought his emotions under control. Eventually, he turned his tear-stained features up to face them. 'There you have it, gentlemen. My tragedy. Her tragedy. Two lives ruined.'

'Where is she now?' asked Ferguson.

'Upstairs. In the attic. Under the covers in a camp bed… I hadn't the heart to bury her.'

Ferguson gave a heavy sigh. 'You'd better show us.'

Brown rose like a man in a trance and led them up a rickety staircase to the top floor. He pointed to the attic door. 'She's in there,' he said.

The room was gloomy, illuminated only by a grimy skylight. There lying on a camp bed was the body of a young woman. The bedclothes were covering her body, but her head was just visible, grey with the pallor of death. Unnervingly her eyes were wide open, staring as though in fright at what they could see on the ceiling.

Only Kishen found his voice to respond to the grim sight. 'It is too, too terrible,' he said softly and retreated from the room. Wilde simply shook his head in sadness, viewing the pale corpse of the young woman, the victim of a sad life and a worse end.

An hour later, they were driving back to London with their prisoner Brown. Ferguson had made several phone calls, and the local Stroud police had taken control of the house and its grisly occupant.

Wilde kept his own counsel during the journey. The day's events had been surprising, to say the least, but they had cleared up one part of the mystery now he was concerned that in following this lead, he had neglected the main one concerning Ambrose De Lacy. He was increasingly worried that this had been a mistake and he had allowed his client to be placed in very imminent danger.

Chapter Thirty-Two

Ambrose De Lacy was about to leave his flat to go for his evening meal when the doorbell rang. His face twisted into a grimace. Who the hell can this be, he thought, wondering whether he should be annoyed or frightened. Surely it couldn't be the phantom letter writer. Or could it?

'Hello,' he called through the door, his hand tentatively holding the latch. He was relieved to hear that response came from a female voice. One he recognised.

His visitor was Meg Granger. She stood at the door shaking in a state of some distress, her face ashen and her eyes moist with tears. 'I must see you,' she gasped, pushing past De Lacy who was stunned by this dramatic entrance. With some apprehension, he followed her into the sitting room. 'What is it, my dear?' he asked in as kindly a tone as he could muster.

'I've come to you for…I'm really not sure. Some advice, I suppose. I don't know who else I could turn to. I have no family or close friends and… well, I suppose the club is my family and… you are the patriarch.'

De Lacy had never thought of himself in this role, and he wasn't sure that the idea pleased him.

Meg unclasped her handbag, withdrew a handkerchief, and dabbed her eyes. 'I have been threatened,' she said quietly, almost a whisper.

De Lacy stiffened at this revelation, and it took all his reserve to appear calm.

'Threatened? In what way?' he asked.

Without replying, Meg's hand reached once more into her handbag and produced a long cream envelope, which she handed to De Lacy.

'I found this pushed through my letter box this morning,' she said.

De Lacy's hands shook as he saw that the envelope simply bore Meg Granger's name written in the same handwriting and purple ink as those cursed ones he had received. Slowly he opened the envelope and withdrew a single sheet of notepaper. His heart constricted as he read the message: 'Your days are numbered. You will die soon.'

The message bore into his brain, and he felt unsteady and sick to the stomach. He had no words at his command to respond to this missive.

'What does it mean?' asked Meg, her voice edged with emotion.

It was some moments before De Lacy spoke. 'It is probably some kind of bizarre joke,' he said with little conviction.

'Joke? They say I'm going to die soon.'

'Who do you think sent it?'

'Gracious, I have no idea.'

'It is probably some crank.'

'Maybe, but a crank who intends to kill me. What should I do?'

De Lacy shook his head. His mind was racing, unsure how to handle this situation. The last thing he wanted was for Granger to go to the police. If she did, it wouldn't be long before they came knocking at his door. That was the last thing he wanted to happen.

'I don't really know...,' he said slowly. 'Perhaps it would be best to ignore it.'

Meg gave a strained unstable laugh. 'Ignore it! How can I do that when my life may be in danger?'

De Lacy gave an exaggerated shrug of the shoulders. 'Why come to me? How do you think I can help you?'

'Because I thought with all your experience... and wisdom you would know what I should do. I mean, should I go to the police, or would they think I was just some hysterical woman...?'

'I wonder if that is wise. After all, it's just one nasty letter. I'm sorry Meg, I'm not being much help. I know I write authoritatively about crime and murder, but it comes from here.' He tapped his forehead. 'I have no experience of such matters in real life. If you don't know of anyone who has a serious grudge against you, I would just…I don't know. Maybe file the letter somewhere, be careful, and if you get another, then go to the police. At least you would have two pieces of evidence to show them.'

Meg stared steadily at De Lacy for a few seconds and then gave a determined nod. 'Yes. Thank you. That is what I will do. It sounds sensible to me. You have been a help to me, Ambrose, and I thank you for it.'

'Well, I believe it is what I would do if I were in your situation,' he lied, giving a gentle smile.

Meg dabbed her eyes and rose from the chair. 'Thank you again. I hope you didn't mind too much my imposing on you in this fashion.'

'No imposition, I assure you. I'm sorry I can't be of more help.'

Meg touched his arm gently and made her way to the door, where she gave De Lacy a hesitant wave before departing without another word.

Straight away, De Lacy headed for the drinks trolley and poured himself a large scotch, which he downed in two gulps. What the hell is going on, his mind raged. Was this demon determined to kill off all the members of the Murder Club? Were none of them safe? His hand instinctively reached for the telephone.

Detective Inspector Johnny Ferguson dropped Wilde and Kishen off at their flat before heading for Scotland Yard with his prisoner, who was, by now, fast asleep in the back of the car, escaping from reality in deep slumber.

The phone was ringing as they entered. 'You'd better take it, Kish, old chap. I am supposed to be dead, remember?'

Kishen flashed a sardonic grin. 'Certainly. We don't want to give any acquaintance of yours a heart attack. A voice from the grave and all that.' The smile disappeared when he heard the frantic voice of Ambrose De Lacy on the line.

'I must see Wilde straight away. It's urgent!'

'Has something happened?'

'Yes. Someone else has been threatened. I must see Wilde.'

'I can arrange that. We'll be with you within the hour.'

'Hurry,' came the strained voice, and then the line went dead.

Kishen passed on the contents of the brief and urgent call to Wilde.

'Let's go,' cried his companion, heading for the door. 'No rest for the wicked.'

De Lacy poured himself another large whisky and began pacing the floor, his mind awhirl with tangled thoughts and his chest taut with tension. What the hell was going on? What was happening to his world? Carfax and Dowson murdered, his life threatened, and now Meg Granger. Who was behind this bloody farrago? He hoped to God that this Wilde fellow could provide some perspective on the matter. Perspective? To hell with that, he wanted him to clear the mystery up, expose the bastard behind it all and return his life to normal: calm waters and sunny days. He snarled at his own conceit. In his perambulations about the flat, he passed the hallway, and something caught his eye. He stopped, frozen in his tracks. It was an envelope lying on the doormat. It wasn't there when Meg Granger had left. With the slow movements of an arthritic marionette, he approached the envelope. He gazed down at it. He saw that it bore his name in that familiar purple ink.

It was from the murderer.

Slowly he bent down and picked it up. With shaky fingers, he tore it open and retrieved the sheet of paper within. He read the message with dread:

'I KNOW WHERE THE BODY IS.'

He staggered backwards, his legs buckling under him. For a moment, he thought he was going to fall down, but instinct caused him to reach out to the wall for support.

Once fully upright, he gave out an agonised moan, the words of the message pounding in his brain: *I know where the body is.*

He stood for some moments, unable to move or think. Gradually, as the shock subsided and rationality began to emerge, he knew what he had to do.

Like a man on fire, he ran to his bedroom and began to pack.

The traffic was bad at that time of day, late afternoon. Wilde and Kishen were snarled up in a jam for some time. Their journey to Granchester Mansions in response to Ambrose De Lacy's desperate summons took much longer than was usual. On reaching his apartment, they rang the bell. Wilde had expected the door to be wrenched open immediately by a sweating, red-faced author, but there was no response. Wilde tried one more time with the same result. He turned a concerned face to his companion. 'I don't like this,' he said.

Kishen leaned forward and tried the door handle with no effect.

'Looks like I'll have to do a little breaking and entering once more.'

Once inside the flat, Wilde called out De Lacy's name, but his cry went unanswered. Swiftly both men searched each of the rooms. There was no sign of the author.

In one respect, Wilde was relieved. One image that had been conjured up by his vivid imagination was the corpse of De Lacy with his head bashed in a similar manner to that of Lord Carfax.

'Looks like the devil has done a bunk,' Wilde observed.

'But why, when he seemed so desperate to talk to you?'

'Obviously, something spooked him after the telephone call.'

'What?'

Wilde shrugged. 'Another call. A visitor, perhaps.'

'A visitor? Maybe the murderer. Has he been kidnapped?'

Wilde shook his head. 'No, there's no sign of violence. I'm fairly certain that he left of his own volition.'

'What makes you say that?'

'The wardrobe door in the bedroom was slightly ajar with several empty hangers, and a suitcase was missing from the top. I saw it there when I was here last on my secret visit.'

Suddenly Wilde seemed distracted, and he wandered over to the wastepaper bin. 'Hello, what do we have here?' He extracted a sheet of paper that had been tightly crumpled into a ball. Gently, he spread it out. 'My, my,' he said to himself before passing the sheet to Kishen.

'Great heavens. 'I know where the body is.' What on earth does that mean?'

'Revenge, Kishen, old boy. It's all about revenge.'

'I'm not sure I understand.'

'I think I'm only seeing things clearly myself. I'll fill you in on the journey.'

'Journey? We're going on a journey? Ah, Cornwall.'

'Yes. Rosemullion Cottage.'

Chapter Thirty-Three

It was moving towards midnight, and yet the erratically flickering dim light set high above in the ceiling was still casting a pale yellow glow, providing the cell with an irritating illumination guaranteed to hinder sleep. But Jacob Brown had no intention of trying to sleep tonight. Or any other night, for that matter.

He sat, foetal like on the edge of the hard metal bed and gazed at his handiwork lying at his feet. Oh, what he would give for a large slug of whisky just now. For a moment, he allowed his mind to wander back to his time with Sadie. Little Sadie. Her face, her sweet, innocent face, rose up in his imagination. Her eyes stared back at him, trusting and simple. Those were the eyes that he had robbed of life. He had snuffed out their light as one might carelessly snuff out a candle. He sobbed at the thought, at the realisation of what he had done. It seemed to him that it was only now, when he had been caught and told his story, that he'd had the ability to take on board the awful fact that he was a murderer. After he had killed Sadie, his main concern, his sole thoughts were to hide her body and pretend to carry on as though nothing had happened. But something had happened, and remorse had landed like a ton weight on his shoulders.

Well, he thought with aching weariness, one cannot change the past, only the future. He had committed the gravest of sins, and he must be punished for it. That was his future, brutal though it may be. But he wasn't going to allow the authorities to carry out the deed in their cold, official objective fashion. It was for him, him alone, to mete out justice. He must pay his own penalty.

Brown reached forward, and from the floor, he pulled up the cotton rope that he had manufactured by carefully tearing his bed sheet into strips and knotting them together. He just hoped that it was strong enough, that it would bear his weight. Instinctively he gazed at the small, barred window high up near the ceiling of the cell. The light bulb had a brief fit, fizzling and crackling as though in erratic tune with his own turbulent emotions.

'Come on, you old bugger,' he murmured to himself. 'Don't prevaricate. Get on with the job.'

Taking hold of the single stool that the cell possessed, he placed it on the bed. It was a little wobbly but, Brown determined, it would have to do its job. It must. Grabbing the makeshift cord, he clambered on to the bed and then carefully mounted the stool. It rocked from side to side, and he almost lost his footing. He bit his lip but made no sound. Having stabilised himself, he reached up to the bars on the window. He had to stand on tiptoe to do so, and again the stool shifted awkwardly. He felt sure it would tip over, sending him crashing to the floor. He froze, remaining stock still for a few seconds, waiting for the bloody stool to behave itself. Once more, he reached up and began threading the end of the improvised rope around one of the bars. Slowly, with infinite patience, he secured one end tightly to the bar.

Now came the really tricky manoeuvre. He wound the other end of the noose around his neck. He wound it around three times, making sure it was as tight as he possibly could. When this was done, he paused, pressing his face against the cold cell wall.

'Well, this is it, old pal,' he said, the words the faintest of whispers. 'You've done wrong, and you must pay. I am so sorry, Sadie.'

With a sudden violent action, he kicked the stool away, and he dropped down, his feet dangling but a few inches above the bed, but that was enough. The rope tightened around his neck. Fireworks exploded before his eyes; his tongue spat out of his mouth along with a deep guttural croak. And then there was darkness, while above the dangling dead body of Jacob Brown, the light bulb continued to splutter and crackle like phantom applause.

Chapter Thirty-Four

It was after midnight when Ambrose De Lacy pulled his car up outside the cottage, the wheels crunching on the pebbles. The headlights illuminated the little whitewashed structure that seemed to spring out of the darkness like a ghost. He switched off the engine and doused the headlights. For some time, he sat gazing at the dark silhouette, while a whole wave of memories washed over him. He found that he was crying: crying for his lost love and crying for himself and the tragedy that he had brought about as a consequence. After a while, he dried his tears and slowly got out of the car, retrieved his case from the boot, and made his way to the front door. Although he was eager to carry out the task he had come all this way for, he knew he would have to wait for daybreak in order to do it and so a sleep on the sofa in the sitting room was his plan. From his coat pocket, he extracted the key that Vivien had given him some time ago and he let himself into the cottage. A musty, stale smell assailed his nostrils as he entered. He switched on a couple of table lamps and made his way to the kitchen to make himself a cup of tea. He needed a little warm sustenance before he tried to go to sleep. He wondered if this was possible. His stomach felt as though a large hand was gripping it, squeezing it tight, and his emotions were all awry. The tea soothed him a little, and he desperately tried to put thoughts of Daniel, the dreaded note, and the purpose of his mission far from his mind. He failed, but tiredness and the fatigue of the long drive gradually overcame all odds, and he slipped into a gentle sleep, curled up on the sofa.

When he awoke, daylight was streaking in through the dusty windows. He sat up with a start. Now, now he could find out. His heart started beating faster, and his head began to ache. For a moment, he was held as though paralysed, unable to move. 'Stop it!' he growled to himself. 'Do the damn thing.'

With an effort, he moved to the hallway and opened a large cupboard situated there. It was where Vivien kept her gardening equipment. He retrieved a spade and walked slowly outside and to the rear of the house, which directly overlooked the sea. The cliff edge was only a hundred feet away. There, placed against the wall of the cottage, was a wooden bench. He gazed at it through misty eyes, and once again, he felt his limbs freeze up. Dropping the spade to the ground, he took hold of one of the arms of the bench and dragged it clear of the wall. He examined the earth where the bench had stood. It seemed flat and undisturbed. Undisturbed, that was the good thing.

I know where the body is.

Like an automaton, he began digging—slowly and carefully. He piled the earth gently to one side as he dug deeper. Eventually, he came to what he was seeking. Lifting a spadeful of earth, he saw the stained sheet he had used as a wrapping. He put the spade aside and stared for quite a time at it, almost expecting it to ripple with movement as its occupant tried to escape its confines. He quickly dismissed this notion from his mind. Dare he reveal its contents? Of course. He knew that he had to. Kneeling down, he scraped away the remaining layer of soil and pulled back the bedsheet. As he did so he gave out a long mournful cry. There he was. Daniel. But Daniel no longer. It was what was left of his love—of his beauty. Creatures had been at him. The face was in tatters. His eyes were missing. For a moment, the line from the old poem came to his mind: 'John Brown's body lies a-mouldering in the grave.' Certainly, his beloved Daniel was mouldering in the grave he had given him. But he hadn't been moved or discovered. So the note that told him, 'I know where the body is' was a hoax. Was a lie! How could anyone know...?

He stood up, still gazing at the thing in the earth with mixed feelings.

'Hello, Ambrose.' A voice came to his ears, floating on the air.

Before he could turn around to face the speaker, he felt a severe pain at the back of his head. As he sank to his knees, he realised he had been struck by some hard instrument. As this thought formed in his mind, he was struck again and lost consciousness.

Chapter Thirty-Five

Rupert Wilde and Kishen Chabra arrived in Falmouth at seven-thirty that morning. 'How do we find exactly where this cottage is?' asked Kishen. 'Coral Point isn't marked on the map.'

'The difficult questions first, eh?' came the response.

'Always.'

'Look, ahead, there is our possible saviour.'

Kishen peered through the windscreen at the solitary figure some distance away, sauntering along the pavement with a canvas sack over his shoulder. 'Ah, Mr Postman.'

'Indeed. Surely he will have some knowledge regarding the exact location of Rosemullion Cottage.'

Wilde was wrong. The postman was a young fellow who had only just moved to this part of the world and had never heard of Coral Point or Rosemullion Cottage. 'My round is Falmouth central, and I'm not overly familiar with it at the moment. Still, I'm learning,' he said cheerfully.

'Thank you anyway,' Wilde said with a tired smile. He was just about to return to the car when the postman stopped him with a hand on the arm. 'I bet I know who would know, though. Barney Groves.'

'And who by the light of the silver moon is Barney Groves?'

'He's a local butcher. And he makes a lot of deliveries to the outlying residents who place regular orders with him. He knows this part of the world like the back of his hand. His shop is only a few streets away. Come on, I'll show you.'

Barney Groves' shop was not open at this early hour, but the man himself was visible behind the counter in his blue and white apron, preparing for the day's business. The postman tapped on the window, attracting Barney's attention. The butcher, a robust fellow with a neat beard and wide brown eyes, grinned a welcome to the familiar figure and went to open the door.

'You got a parcel for me, Sam?' he said in a broad Cornish accent.

'No, it's these two gents here are wanting to know how to get to Rosemullion Cottage on Coral Point.'

Barney screwed up his face. 'Rosemullion? Miss Dowson's place. But she ain't there at the moment. She always rings me up with her order before she comes down. I ain't heard a dicky bird from her for weeks.'

'We're friends of hers,' said Wilde stepping forward. 'We're renting the place from her for a while.'

'Are you now?'

'We're writers, too,' added Kishen with a smile.

'Didn't she give you instructions how to get there herself?' Barney asked, narrowing his eyes.

Wilde nodded. 'Yes, but like fools, we forgot to bring them with us. Can you help?'

The butcher paused for a moment, scrutinising their faces. 'I suppose so,' Barney said with some reluctance, stepping out of the shop on to the pavement. He stuck his left arm out, pointing down the street. 'Coral Point is in that direction, some five miles.' And he continued to give detailed directions, which both Wilde and Kishen noted carefully. Thanking Barney and the postman for their assistance, they hurried back to the car.

The sun was sending broad yellow lines across the sea, as Wilde and Kishen motored down the rough unmade track towards the solitary cottage which, in the early morning light seemed to be teetering on the edge of the cliff.

'Look, there's a car by the front door. De Lacy's I'll be bound.'

'So, you were right. He did come here.'

'It would seem so.'

Wilde parked behind the other car. 'Right, let's investigate.'

The door of the cottage was unlocked, and on entering the sitting room, they saw a small suitcase and an overcoat. 'That is Mr De Lacy's,' observed

Kishen.

'Yes, there's his coat, but where the devil is he?' They searched all the rooms but there was no sign of the man himself.

'That's very strange,' said Kishen.

'Mmm. Let's have a look outside.'

Eventually, they found the body of Ambrose De Lacy lying on the ground at the rear of the cottage. Nearby was a shallow hole which, to their horror, contained human remains. It was a corpse in a nightmarish state of decomposition. Kishen turned his head away as his stomach retched at the grisly sight. 'What on earth has been going on here?' he asked.

'Revenge. I believe we have solved the mystery of the disappearance of Daniel Collins.'

'Great heavens! And De Lacy... is he dead?

'I think so.' Wilde knelt down and took De Lacy's wrist. 'There's no pulse. Oh, wait a minute...I think there's a faint... Great heavens, yes.' At this moment, the author's eyes flickered open briefly.

Wilde gave a gasp of surprise. 'The old devil is still alive. Just.'

Kishen gazed down at De Lacy in wonderment. He had obviously been savagely attacked and beaten about his head, which lay in a thick pool of blood. His mouth was twisted awkwardly as though frozen in the process of emitting a scream. How could this man still be in the land of the living?

As though Wilde had read his companion's thoughts said quietly, 'I reckon he will not last much longer. Have a look in the house, Kishen, see if there is a cushion, a blanket, and some brandy to give him. If we can revive him briefly, perhaps he can tell us what happened.'

When Kishen returned with a bottle of brandy, he saw that Wilde had lifted De Lacy's body up into a sitting position, resting him against the old wooden bench. Remarkably the author's eyes were open. Kishen tried to make him comfortable while Wilde administered the brandy, which De Lacy imbibed like a baby.

'Who did this to you?' he asked.

A faint shake of the head. 'Didn't see.' The voice was faint and tortured, his chest rattling as he spoke.

'You came here to see if Daniel's grave had been discovered.'

De Lacy closed his eyes again and issued a whispered moan as tears made rivulets down the blood on his cheeks. 'Yes. 'How much do you know?'

'Enough to know that you are a murderer and were being targeted for your crime,' said Wilde.

De Lacy groaned again.

'Come on, De Lacy, you are the author,' said Wilde harshly. 'Tell me your story.'

With painful slowness and wheezing breath, De Lacy wiped the tears away with his sleeve and gazed for some moments at the shadowed features of two men standing over him. 'More brandy, first,' he said.

And then, in a halting, tortured manner with many pauses to catch his failing breath and to be sustained temporarily by brandy, Ambrose De Lacy revealed his dark confession.

Chapter Thirty-Six

Ambrose De Lacy's story

Daniel was the real love of my life. I adored him. On meeting him, it was the first time in my life that I felt genuine affection for another human being. I know this sounds dramatic, but something stirred within my breast when I met him. Oh, yes, he was young and beautiful, but it was more than that. There was a certain magic in his personality that enchanted me, engrossed me. I didn't know then that most of it was a performance. Nevertheless, I loved him, and I thought he cared for me. But as it turned out, I was wrong. We became lovers, physical lovers, and I was completely taken in by his supposed passionate affection for me. I was so captivated, obsessed with my Daniel that I was blind to his deception.

It was only at the end that I learned how he had used me. I suppose I was foolish in the way that I spoiled him, but that's what you do when you care deeply for someone and, besides, I was in a position to do it. He borrowed money from me, and he promised that he would pay it back. I think we both knew that he wouldn't. But I didn't care. I knew he was a reckless individual where finances were concerned. He was reckless in other ways, too. That was part of his attraction for me. And like the foolish old man I was, I showered him with gifts, cufflinks, pearl tie pins, a silver cigarette case. I suppose I was, if you like, trying to buy him, to keep him by my side. I was so infatuated and terrified that he would leave me for someone else.

He was due to go into the army, or so he led me to believe, and just before that was about to happen, we came here for what I believed would be a very romantic break before our parting when he went to France. I was desperately unhappy at the prospect of being without him, but I was determined that this would be a wonderful and memorable time together.

It all started well, and then on the first night, Daniel over indulged with wine and became argumentative and brusque. When I went to him, to try to calm him down, to kiss him, he rejected my embrace and pushed me away, shouting, 'Get away, you old fool.' I had never seen him like that before. He had become someone else. He glared at me with such ferocity. There really was hatred in his eyes. I was mortified. It was as though he had stuck a knife in my heart. He could see that I was distraught—I had begun to cry a little—and that made him worse. He laughed at me and said some horrible things—things, no doubt, he had been harbouring in his mind from the start. He told me his relationship with me had been a game to see how far he could go with me. How much he could deceive me. To use his expression: 'How much I could fool the old fool.' He had been laughing behind my back all along while I had given him cash, bought him expensive presents, paid for his dinners, his tailor's bill, and gambling debts. He had used me, ridiculed me, and taken my genuine affection for him and trodden it in the dirt.

The more I grew upset by his revelations, the more he laughed. And then, his hideous bray caused me to snap. Suddenly the self-pity that had engulfed me was replaced by anger, by rage. It fired up within me. All affection turned to hate. I wanted to smash that sneering, beautiful face. As he sat back in his drunken stupor, chuckling to himself, I grabbed the poker from the hearth and….

Well, you can guess what I did. I can still hear the cracking of his skull as the poker smashed into him. It was the worst moment of my life. I… I killed him with one blow. The man I had loved lay at my feet, a bloodied corpse.

My mind was paralysed at first. I just kept staring down at his once handsome features, now smeared with blood. I could hardly believe the terrible act I had just committed. I really didn't mean to kill him. Just hurt him, hurt him badly as he had hurt me. I just….

Eventually, I pulled myself together and dragged his body outside and, covering him with a sheet, I dug a grave…where he still lies….

Chapter Thirty-Seven

'...I dug a grave...where he still lies.'

As De Lacy spoke these words, his body shuddered as though invisible hands were gently shaking it, and then with an eerie expiration of air, the author's eyes closed for the last time.

Wilde took the man's wrist for a moment and then shook his head. Both he and Kishen stared in silence for some time at the dead man.

'It is a terrible story,' said Kishen at length.

'One that is not yet complete, I'm afraid.'

Kishen nodded. 'Yes, of course. There is still De Lacy's murderer at large. We must assume that it is Wilfred Collins who sought revenge for his brother's death.'

It was just after noon, and he and Wilde were motoring back to London after a busy morning sorting out the mess at Rosemullion Cottage. Wilde had driven into Falmouth to inform the local police of the situation as well as contacting Johnny Ferguson at the Yard. Kishen had stayed behind as 'guardian of the dead' as he referred to it. Within an hour a number of policemen, uniformed officers, and a forensic team were swarming all over the property. Satisfied that everything was being handled efficiently, Wilde and Kishen set off back to London to 'finally clear up this nasty business' as Wilde noted.

'I know that it would seem logical and obvious that Wilfred was De Lacy's murderer. A mentally disturbed man on the run.'

'And you think that he must have guessed what had happened at Rosemullion.'

'I don't think he guessed. I believe he knew.'

'If that is the case, it certainly seems that De Lacy's murder was as I assumed an act of revenge, but—'

'Indeed…there is a but.'

Kishen frowned. 'You are not making sense, Rupert. What are you thinking?'

Wilde remained silent for a time before responding. His reply did not really answer Kishen's question. 'We certainly have to discover the whereabouts of Wilfred and do that pronto.'

'How are we going to do that?'

'Well, for a start, I think that when we reach London, we must pay a call on a certain lady.'

Some hours later, Wilde parked the car in a narrow tree-lined road in Islington. 'Here we are,' he said with a smile.

'Here we are… where?' asked Kishen.

'Sandford Road. And we are looking for Tarragon Villa, the home of the crime writer Meg Granger. Remember I managed to get details of her address with my little subterfuge in Strong's office at Blackstone books.'

'Yes, I remember. But why are we here now?"

'To get to the truth.'

Sandford Road was a thoroughfare of mixed properties: some smart and elegant, others having seen better times. Tarragon Villa was of the smart and elegant variety, with a small pretty garden at the front filled with a range of bright flowers, which waved as a gentle variegated sea of colour in the evening breeze. It was in direct contrast to the property next door, with its proliferation of weeds and scrubby lawn. This did not seem to bother the fellow sitting on the porch in a wicker chair reading the newspaper. He was a gaunt individual with thinning grey hair and a sallow complexion.

As Wilde and Kishen made their way up the path to the front door, the man barely gave them a glance. Wilde rang the doorbell. There was no response.

'Perhaps the lady is out,' said Kishen.

'Maybe,' said Wilde pressing the bell again, allowing his finger to linger on the button for longer than was polite.

This time they heard sound beyond the door. And then there was a voice. 'Who is there?' it said.

'Someone who knows your secret,' said Wilde. 'It would be in your interest to let us in; otherwise, I cannot be responsible for the consequences.'

There was a long pause and the sound of a key turning in the lock. The door opened, and Meg Granger stood before them. Her face registered shock when she saw Wilde standing before her.

'You!' she said.

'Yes, it's me. Returned from the grave, don't y'know. How lovely to see you again, Miss Granger or, should I say, Bolly.'

She gave a cry of surprise and instinctively attempted to close the door, but Wilde took a step forward and held the door open firmly.

'I do think it is best if we come in for a talk.'

For a moment Meg Granger did not move. She just stood there staring at the two men with a blank expression on her face. At length she spoke, her voice a strained, strangled whisper. 'I don't know what the hell this is all about but, if you must, come in, and let's get it over with quickly.'

She led them into the sitting room and, with a curt wave of the hand, indicated that they should sit, but both men remained standing. She moved to a drinks trolley and poured herself a large glass of wine and then turned defiantly to face them.

'So, Mr Wilde, what is the reason for this intrusion?' she said, with a certain arrogance, indicating to Wilde that her self-confidence was returning.

'I was hoping that I could extract a confession from you.'

'A confession. For what?'

'For the murders of Lord Carfax, Vivien Dowson, and Ambrose De Lacy.'

Again, she froze, her features betraying no emotion and then suddenly she threw her head back and laughed. It was like the laugh of a squawking parrot. 'Are you mad? I thought I was the one who came up with preposterous plots for my novels. I see now that I have some competition.'

'Your name is not Meg Granger, but Susan Margaret Collins. You were foolish enough to use your full name in the visitors' book when you visited Brandwell. Dr Mellor informed me of this fact. You are the sister of Daniel and Wilfred Collins, an identity you disposed of some years ago. You kept the Margaret but shortened it to Meg and adopted a new surname.'

She opened her mouth to speak, but Wilde held up his hand to prevent her. 'Please don't deny it, Bolly.'

At Wilde's use of this name, the woman flinched. 'That was the pet name your brothers gave you, wasn't it?'

She said nothing and just took a drink of wine.

'Bolly. Probably based on your early taste for Bollinger champagne. Indeed, I see a bottle on your drinks trolley even now.'

'What sharp little eyes you have. But that does not prove a thing, really. Does it?'

'By itself, of course not. Where is Wilfred now?'

'I'm sorry, I don't know what you are talking about.'

'Once again, my sharp little eyes have been at work. The framed picture on the mantelpiece. The young chap in the uniform, that's Wilfred, isn't it? He's the fellow you visited at Brandwell isn't he?'

Meg Granger sat on the arm of the sofa and took another swig of wine before replying. 'Do go on, Mr Wilde. All this is a most fascinating fiction.'

'My dear Bolly, you have been living a lie for some time, haven't you? Writing a crime novel while you were convalescing.'

'Well, you've got that right, at least.'

'And from what were you convalescing? I would suggest you were under supervision for some kind of mental illness.'

'I think not!' She was angry now, and her hand shook so vigorously that wine spilled over the lip of the glass.

'You have suffered from mental problems since your youth and I believe that it was this unstable condition that has led you to this terrible trail of murder. No doubt it was the death or rather the murder of your other brother Daniel that tipped you over the edge. You knew that Ambrose De Lacy killed him. And so you sought revenge.'

At the mention of De Lacy's name, a strange transformation took hold of Meg Granger. She rose to her feet, her face contorted with suppressed fury, and she threw her wine glass into the fireplace.

'That man is vermin,' she roared. 'He snuffed out the life of my sweet brother….'

'Your sweet brother who attempted to blackmail De Lacy. But his plan backfired, didn't it? De Lacy retaliated and killed Daniel.'

Meg Granger had now begun to cry, but she wiped away the tears with a savage gesture, brushing her forearm across her face.

'I assume you knew of Daniel's plan to blackmail De Lacy,' said Wilde.

This remark brought a guttural laugh. 'Knew? Of course, I did. It was my idea. I planned it. All to help my brother. I worked it out for him, and he played the game like a champion. He compromised the old fool. He carefully gathered evidence, as well as a bit of cash on the way. We both knew that the denouement was imminent. The invitation to that cursed cottage in Cornwall seemed the ideal time to bring down the curtain on this delicious plan. It was time for De Lacy to learn the truth. He had to be told that he had been duped and he would have to pay dearly for his foolishness. De Lacy never stopped to think for one moment why a beautiful man like Daniel would get involved with that narcissistic old bag of bones, so gullible was he. When Daniel didn't return from that weekend, I knew something was wrong. I went down to the cottage, and it didn't take me long to work out what had happened. I felt sure my dear brother had lost his life there, but I didn't know where he was buried…until yesterday.'

'Tell me, Miss Granger,' said Kishen taking a step forward, 'if you knew that Mr De Lacy had murdered Daniel, why didn't you take your revenge on him immediately? Why murder these other people?'

Meg Granger giggled. 'For fun,' she said. 'Killing the old devil straight away was too easy. I wanted to unnerve him, to make him terrified for a while. In simple terms, I wanted to fry his brain with fear. He had to suffer first before death. I took joy in letting him know that the Grim Reaper was on his way, but not quite yet. I wanted to treat the old buzzard to the agony of anticipation. I overheard that fool Carfax threaten him, so I thought he was a likely victim—an hors d'ouevre if you like to the main banquet. It was very pleasing to despatch the drunken buffoon.' She giggled again, her eyes misting as though picturing the scene of Carfax's demise. 'His death really put the wind up De Lacy. Mission accomplished.' The giggle now turned into a dark unstable laugh.

'And Vivien Dowson?' prompted Wilde.

'Ah, old Viv. Well, there was more purpose behind her demise. It was she who provided the means and location for Daniel's murder. If she had not let De Lacy use her blasted Rosemullion, maybe my darling brother would still be alive.'

'It is a tenuous motive.'

'So? What's wrong with a tenuous motive? I thrive on tenuous motives.' She laughed loudly again, and both men realised she was actually enjoying herself discussing, as she saw things, the success of her bloody machinations.

'I need another drink,' she said, moving swiftly to the drinks trolley and pouring herself another large glass of wine.

'A final touch,' she said grandly, after downing half the glass in one gulp, 'a final touch was visiting the terrified toad and telling him that I had received a threatening letter, too.' More laughter. 'That really confused the bastard.'

'And then you sent him a note prompting him to go back to Rosemullion.'

'He was by now so riddled with guilt and fear, that I knew if I suggested that his nemesis knew where he had buried Daniel, he would go and check. And he did.'

'You followed him down to Cornwall.'

'I did and saw him dig up Daniel's corpse….' Now there was a sudden change in her demeanour. The light of humour that had flared in her eyes died away, and tears came. Her body shook with emotion as she emptied her glass. 'My poor dear boy. There he lay… His remains…' She let out an agonised cry and slumped down in a chair. 'It all became real then. The whole sorry saga. Something within me told me that… well, all my plotting and crimes had been in vain. That my revenge was in vain. Nothing… nothing would bring my baby brother back. There he lay in a makeshift pit, eaten by worms, ragged remnants of flesh, blank eye sockets. Dead.'

CHAPTER THIRTY-SEVEN

'And yet you killed De Lacy.'

'Oh, yes. Oh, yes. I had to, you see. To complete my task. The Bible has something to say about such things, doesn't it? An eye for an eye. I struck him down as he had struck Daniel down. It was just, but I have to admit it has not brought me the peace I expected. I now see that nothing will, and so I'm content to pay my dues. I really have no other purpose in life. I avenged my brother's death—that gives me some sort of comfort but not rest or contentment.'

'And what of your other brother, Wilfred?'

'Poor Wilfred. The war did for him, you know. He had a fine mind and a gentle soul, but his experience in France tore down his fragile structures of rationality. Everywhere he turned, he saw dark threatening shadows.'

'You know where he is?'

Her face brightened again. 'Wouldn't you like to know.'

'Yes. That's about the long and short of it. No doubt you assisted his departure, shall we call it, from Brandwell, planned on your visits to him there.'

'No doubt,' she murmured, with a dark smile.

'On his escape, did Wilfred come back here?'

'You are a smart little detective, aren't you?'

'I try to be.'

'Well, I reckon you'll be on a hiding to nothing in trying to find Wilfred.'

'Why so?'

'Because even I don't know where he is now. Certainly, I gave him advice, instructions how to leave that sanitised prison camp. If you weren't crazy before you passed through the portals of Brandwell, you would be within a month incarcerated there. Thank God, I got Willy out. He came here for a few days, but we both knew he couldn't stay. It wouldn't be long before the police came sniffing around my house. My brother had now become some kind of frail stranger, frightened of his own shadow. If you must know, I got him to France. Boat train to Paris, away from the reach of Brandwell and the British authorities. As I waved him goodbye at the station, that pale face and haunted eyes gazing back at me, I knew that would be the last time I saw my brother. It was. I have no idea where he is now, and perhaps I don't want to know. At least he's not in Brandwell. At least he is physically free, if not mentally so.'

She gave a deep sigh and poured herself another drink, which she consumed in one swift gulp. 'So, what now, Mr Detective and his swarthy friend? Are you going to arrest me?'

'Indeed, I think it is best that you come along with us to Scotland Yard,' said Wilde softly.

'Why not? I've had my fun. And the old devil is dead.' She laughed and staggered a little, but Wilde saw that her erratic movements were faked. In an instant, she had made for the door of the sitting room. She was through it in an instant, but Wilde was close behind. Meg Granger headed for the kitchen and slammed the door shut.

To his horror, Wilde had a notion of what the woman was planning to do. He tried to open the door, but it resisted. She must have propped a chair up against the handle, he deduced. He had to get into the room quickly, or it would be too late. He stood back, and with all his might, he kicked hard against the door. It flew open. He rushed into the room. There was Meg Granger standing by the sink, holding a sharp kitchen knife over her left wrist.

'No,' cried Wilde. 'That is not the answer.'

'It is the *only* answer,' screamed Meg Granger.

Just then, an object flew past Wilde. It was a wine glass thrown by Kishen. It crashed on the floor, splintering into many pieces. It landed at Meg Granger's feet. Temporarily distracted by this sudden unexpected event, she lost her concentration. It gave Wilde time enough to leap forward and snatch the knife from her hand. With a groan, she collapsed to the floor.

A little time later, a police car arrived to take Meg Granger to Scotland Yard. As she was led down the path of her house by two uniformed officers, her next-door neighbour, who was still sitting on the porch, glanced up from his newspaper, a gentle frown of curiosity creasing his brow. 'I wonder,' he mused, 'where those men are taking my sister.'

Chapter Thirty-Eight

Within the hour, Meg Granger was in the hands of the officials at Scotland Yard. All the fight and the fury in her nature had evaporated. It was as though in telling her story, admitting her crimes to Wilde and Kishen, a burden had been lifted from her soul. 'I am content now,' she told Wilde, as she was led away by a uniformed officer. 'One brother revenged; one brother free. I am satisfied. I do not care for myself.'

After she had gone, Wilde and Kishen stood for some time in silence. 'You know,' said Wilde, at length, 'I cannot help feeling sorry for the woman. I know she has carried out a series of heinous crimes, but in her mind, her troubled, unstable mind, they were acts of justice. She is not an inherently evil creature, just a misguided one.'

'Indeed,' agreed Kishen. 'The mind is responsible for controlling all our actions, both good and bad. It is clear that all the Collins siblings were in some way tainted with mental issues. As someone once said, 'There but for the grace of God, go I.'

'It's a damn sobering thought, ain't it?' said Wilde, patting his companion on the back. 'Come on, old chap, let's hightail it to the Yard. There will be statements to make.'

'I had planned for a quiet evening, contemplating my navel while consuming a fair few glasses of the hard stuff. Trust you to drag me back to the office to deal with the detritus of this awful case.' The twinkle in Inspector Johnny Ferguson's eyes and the gentle smile resting on his lips belied the grumpiness of his declaration.

It was some hours later, and Wilde and Kishen were ensconced in Ferguson's office at Scotland Yard. Meg Granger had been cautioned, a statement taken, and was, for the moment, spending the night in a cell. After her bravado back at the house, she now seemed docile, resigned to her fate. There was no fight left in her, merely signs of relief. Relief that it was all over; relief that she had been caught. She had, after all, achieved her main goal, the killing of Ambrose De Lacy, an act she saw not as murder but as justified revenge for ending the life of her beloved brother, Daniel.

'Well,' said Wilde languidly, 'I knew that you'd like to be in at the finale. It was your investigation as much as mine in the end.'

Ferguson nodded. 'Yes, of course. So now that most of the immediate paperwork has been sorted out, why don't you give me an overview of the case from your point of view. It will help me when I have to write up my official report on the matter.'

In a detailed fashion, Wilde covered all the points of the story, blending the details of De Lacy's confession with that of Meg Granger's. 'It would seem,' he said, 'that she had a particular facility for male disguise. My friend Sally was convinced that the person who abducted her was a man—granted, a strange man, but nevertheless, a man.'

'It seems,' observed Kishen 'that she applied all the imaginative skill she used in her fiction in this real game of terror and murder.'

'Yes,' agreed Wilde. 'I suppose there is a thin line between inspired imagination and inspired madness. Sadly, she crossed it.'

'I understand that and, from what you tell me,' said Ferguson, 'it is very likely she will escape the gallows and....'

'End up in an institution like Brandwell.' Wilde completed his sentence. 'There is a cruel irony in such a fate.'

There was a long pause during which no one spoke, and then Wilde gave a large sigh. 'Well, he said, 'the case is closed, although it doesn't give me a great deal of satisfaction. If only De Lacy had been honest with me at the start, then perhaps....'

'But he couldn't do that without incriminating himself,' said Kishen.

Wilde nodded. 'Time to go and wash the unpleasantness of this case away with a very dry martini. Although I suspect it will take more than one.'

'Before you leave, Rupert, I'm afraid I have some further unpleasant news. It's about Jacob Brown.'

It was midnight when Wilde and Kishen returned to the flat. Wilde was not drunk but certainly less than sober. He slumped down in an easy chair and lit a cigarette.

'Black coffee?' suggested Kishen.

Wilde gave a half smile. 'Why not.'

He was on his second cigarette when coffee arrived. 'I cannot help feeling I did rather badly in this case, Kishen, old friend.'

'Nonsense,' came the stern reply. 'You identified the culprit and brought her to justice.'

'After a string of corpses.'

'Because you had very little to go on. Without your efforts, no doubt the murderer would have got away with it—and who knows if she'd not take it into her mind to set forth on another killing spree in the future. You were dealing with an unstable mind where logic is somewhat at a disadvantage.'

Wilde chuckled. 'You have the smooth persuasiveness of a politician.'

'Mr Wilde, if you are going to insult me in such a manner, I shall retire for the night.'

Both men laughed.

Chapter Thirty-Nine

A few days later, Rupert Wilde was having lunch with Sally Peters in a little café off the Strand. It was at her invitation. On this occasion, she was at their table before Wilde. As he made his way across the room and caught sight of Sally, he saw that she wore a serious almost apprehensive expression. He hoped that he was imagining it.

She leant forward to give him a kiss on the cheek as he sat down. 'How are you, and how's the case?' she asked.

'I'm fine, and the case is closed. It's all over and done with, but I really don't want to talk about it. I would much prefer to hear all your news. How was Brighton?'

She smiled. 'It was pleasant enough. But one can have too much of a good thing. I'm afraid my aunt can talk one's ear off. It comes from living alone, I suppose, and having no one to converse with regularly. Don't get me wrong, she's a lovely lady, but…. And to be honest, I got a little homesick.'

'So now you're back and have resumed your old life, eh?'

'Pretty much so. And I have to say—'

'You're happy that way.'

Sally paused. 'Yes, I am happy that way. I had time—lots of time—in Brighton to think. To think about us.'

'What did you think?'

'Well, I came to a decision. It wasn't easy but, in the end, I think it was a sensible one.'

Wilde could see the way this was going but said nothing.

'That night. The kidnap. The fire. It was awful. Frightening. I still have

196

some bruises….'

Wilde could see that Sally was struggling and took her hand and squeezed it gently.

'Your life, your dangerous life, is so different from mine,' she said. 'It is unsettling and…oh, I don't know. I am close to caring for you too much, but I would be in constant fear for your safety, never knowing if you would come home in one piece or even come home at all. It simply isn't the life for me.'

'My dear Sally, you don't have to say any more. I know what you mean. And if it's any consolation, I also understand and agree.'

'If only you were a doctor or an architect—or even a bus driver. But a detective with danger and crime ready to engulf you at any time.'

Wilde smiled. 'I know, and if I had any talent to be a doctor, architect, or even a bus driver, I'd have a go, but I don't.'

'So, you see what I am saying.'

'Yes, of course, and you are right. In our short acquaintance, I have become fond of you—so fond, in fact, not to want to drag you into my uncertain world. You deserve better, something more serene.'

'Yes, more serene certainly, but I doubt if I'll find better, my dear Rupert.'

She leaned forward and gave him a warm kiss on the lips.

After the meal, they left the café and said their goodbyes. They hugged and kissed for the last time before going separate ways. Wilde walked up the Strand to Trafalgar Square and stared at the gushing fountains for some time. Sally was right, he mused. While his time with her had been a brief but wonderful interlude, he knew that his life, his detective work, would always have got in the way of their romance, and that would not be fair on her. Sad but true. So, what had the bachelor detective got to look forward to now? He allowed himself a brief smile. 'The next case, of course.'

About the Author

David Stuart Davies is an author, playwright and editor. He has written nine Sherlock Holmes novels and *Starring Sherlock Holmes,* which details the film career of the famous sleuth. He has also created detective series set variously in London during World War II, New York in the 1930s and 1980s Yorkshire. His non-fiction work *Bending the Willow: Jeremy Brett as Sherlock Holmes* is regarded as the definitive work on the subject.

Currently, he is the general contributing editor for Wordsworth Editions Mystery & Supernatural series. He is an invested Baker Street Irregular, and a member of The Detection Club. He has given talks and dramatic presentations on crime fiction and his collections of ghost stories at various literary festivals, libraries, and conferences as well on the Queen Mary II. His first Rupert Wilde Mystery, *The Dead of Winter*, was published by Level Best Books in 2022.

SOCIAL MEDIA HANDLES:
  Twitter: @DStuartDavies

AUTHOR WEBSITE:

davidstuartdavies.co.uk

Also by David Stuart Davies

RUPERT WILDE NOVELS:
  The Dead of Winter

SHERLOCK HOLMES NOVELS:
  Sherlock Holmes & the Hentzau Affair
  The Tangled Skein
  The Veiled Detective
  The Shadow of the Rat
  The Scroll of the Dead
  The Devil's Promise
  The Ripper Legacy
  The Instrument of Death
  Revenge from the Grave

JOHNNY HAWKE NOVELS:
  Forests of the Night
  Comes the Dark
  Without Conscience
  Requiem for a Dummy
  The Darkness of Death
  A Taste for Blood
  Spiral of Lies

THE PAUL SNOW TRILOGY:
  Brothers in Blood
  Innocent Blood
  Blood Rites

OTHER NOVELS
  Oliver Twist and the Mystery of Throate Manor

The Scarlet Coven
The Darkness Rising

SUPERNATURAL COLLECTIONS:
The Halloween Mask
In the Shadows

NON-FICTION:
Holmes of the Movies
Starring Sherlock Holmes
Bending the Willow: Jeremy Brett as Sherlock Holmes
The Sherlock Holmes Book (co-edited with Barry Forshaw)